Absolution of Fate

S. Simone Chavous

Proofreading by Kimberly Huther of Wordsmith Proofreading

ISBN: 978-0-9895701-5-2
eISBN: 978-0-9895701-4-5

Visit my website: http://www.ssimonechavous.com

Like me on Facebook: http://www.facebook.com/ssimonechavous

Follow me on Twitter: http://www.twitter.com/ssimonechavous

To all my readers, for sticking it out to the end.

Contents

CHAPTER 1 - *The Aftermath*

Ethan remained frozen, watching with eyes full of rage and torment as the woman who he'd known as a little girl only weeks before disappeared into the mist with a monster. With her went the last piece of his fragmented heart. Feeling the distance between him and his master grow, he let out a heavy breath and dropped to his knees. The weight of the past week's events pressed down on him like a two-ton boulder. He bowed his head and let the pain wash over and cover him like a blanket of fire. In his mind, he deserved it all; he'd brought the wrath of a madman down upon everyone he loved. All because he was selfish enough to believe he had the power to defy fate, to change what was written in the stars. For his vanity, he was punished. He understood that now.

He could hear The Elite soldiers stirring inside but, as commanded, he laid down his weapons and waited. He secretly hoped it wouldn't matter that he had laid down his arms, that they would see him for the monster he was end his miserable existence. He had nothing left; nothing but hate and the bone-deep desire to remove Lucias's head from his shoulders.

He'd completely forgotten about Layla standing beside him until he heard her weapons hit the concrete. Like him, she was merely obeying the last command Lucias had given. Ethan looked at her as she stared out across the grounds, her face blank; completely devoid of any emotion and he wondered if she was like him. Was the person she used to be still trapped inside, constantly screaming commands at a body which was deaf to the sound, listening only to the call of its new master's blood? Or had she let go and given herself over completely to the beast inside, no longer feeling guilt or remorse, instead just functioning on primal need and obedience. He'd looked into her eyes that night in Lucias's playroom; he knew it was the latter and he almost envied her for it. Holding on to his humanity was the reason he suffered, but he would never completely let go. He couldn't; Alexa wouldn't want him to and, though she was gone, he refused to let her down again.

"GET ON YOUR KNEES!"

Both he and Layla obeyed the command shouted from the front door.

"Hands behind your head!"

The instant it was done, three Elite, armed to the teeth, appeared several yards in front of them. The heartbeats behind him let Ethan know there were five more there.

"Oh fuck; it's Layla and they're infected!" one of the men shouted with his weapon aimed between Ethan's eyes. "Get cuffs on them now," the same soldier said. "If either of you move a millimeter, we will put you down...permanently," he hissed.

Both Ethan and Layla remained perfectly still as the silver handcuffs were locked on in a blur of motion behind them. Neither one even flinched as the cold metal burned into their infected skin. A second later, two loud pops sounded and Ethan felt a dart pinch his neck. While it wasn't enough to knock an infected vampire out completely, he swayed forward as the tranquilizer spread through his body.

"Get them both to the confinement wing now, and put them where they won't be seen," Commander Claesson ordered, stepping through the doorway. He paused, grabbing the doorjamb as his legs wobbled beneath him, a lingering effect of Chloe's power.

With the powerful sedative pulsing through their veins, neither Ethan nor Layla struggled as the guards dragged them away. Of course, with Lucias's last command, even if they wanted to resist there was no way they could.

"Until we figure out what we're dealing with, no one, and I mean no one is to have any contact with those two," Claesson whispered to one of his captains just before a group of Elite soldiers returning from patrol led by Dante sped across the lawn.

"Where is she?" Dante demanded, stopping only inches away from the Commander.

"Stand down, soldier," Commander Claesson replied, knowing it was pointless to deny that Layla was back on the compound. Her undeniable scent clung to the humid air around them. Instead, he used every ounce of his slowly-returning strength to stand to his full height as he faced Dante's wrath.

"She's safe, but understand me, soldier, no one, including you is to have any contact with either of the prisoners without my approval."

"So Layla's a fucking prisoner now?" Dante responded, practically pushing his chest into the Commander in challenge.

The Commander sighed, but he didn't back down a millimeter. "She's infected, Dante. I know she means a lot to you, but until we figure out exactly what we're dealing with, both Layla and Ethan are off-limits."

Dante stumbled back as the reality of what the Commander said seemed to knock all the air from his lungs.

Martinez was behind him in an instant, catching his friend's full weight before he fell to the ground. With the hypersensitive hearing possessed by all of his kind, he'd heard everything. He wanted to tell Dante it would be all right, that she would be all right, but like everyone else, he knew what being infected meant.

Alexa slowly opened her eyes, feeling a bit disoriented as she pushed up from the cold floor of the training room. The others remained unconscious on the floor around her. Though she already knew that Chloe was gone, her maternal eyes darted around in search of her only daughter. The visions Chloe had shared were suddenly fresh in her mind as she moved to the door, desperate to find Ethan. Even without the benefit of Chloe's clairvoyance, Alexa knew that Ethan was close by; she could feel him as surely as if his arms were around her.

She moved on unsteady legs towards the door, feeling stronger with each step. The minds around her began to stir, the sounds reminding her of a car engine trying to turn after sitting idle on a cold winter's night. She reached for her father's mind, searching for the security code before he was aware enough to erect his mental shields again. The panel light flashed green and Alexa was at the entrance to the residential wing before the door had even resealed. She moved with a speed she didn't know she possessed, using only her bond with Ethan to guide her. She felt him growing closer with each step and her heart was swelling with elated anticipation; until she rounded the last corner.

"I'm sorry ma'am; no one is permitted through this door until further notice. Commander's orders," a soldier whose name she didn't know drawled.

"Let me pass; I know my husband is in there," Alexa demanded, full of determination to get to the man she loved.

"Alexa." She turned to face Dante as he approached; his eyes full of agony that seemed to ease slightly at the sight of her. "I wouldn't bother; he couldn't let you pass if he wanted to. They've engaged the maximum security protocol. Only Commander Claesson can open that door now," he stated as he pulled her into his arms to comfort himself as much as her. She relaxed into him, suddenly feeling the strain from the exertion of moving so quickly before she'd had a chance to fully recover from Chloe's mind blast. While intimate, the embrace was only one of friendship and comfort.

"Come, you need to feed," Dante said sensing Alexa's weakness and leading her away. As a mirror, the longer her held on to her, the stronger his reflection of her psychic ability became. Though her mental shields were in place, he could still read her feelings.

"But I need to see him. He needs to see me alive; he's in so much pain," Alexa plead, her eyes welling up with tears of frustration and exhaustion.

"I know; I want to get in there as badly as you do. Layla's with him and she's been infected, too, but there's nothing we can do for them until the doctors find a cure."

"No, I can save him! Chloe showed me before she left, we need to renew our mate bond; it will free him," Alexa said with desperation.

"What do you mean Chloe *left*?" Dante asked stopping. He turned her to face him and grabbed her shoulders.

"She went with Lucias, to save us; to save all of us. There were so many infected, we all would have died. She had a vision of it before they came. She gave herself up to keep us safe."

"How could Claesson let her do that? How could *you*?" Dante asked, sounding more judgmental than he'd intended.

"I didn't let her do anything!" Alexa snapped. "She knocked everyone out and left, but not before she showed me what I needed to do to save her father; so like I said, I need to see him now!"

"I know Claesson; he's not going to let you in, vision or no vision. It's too much of a risk to the rest of the compound. If an infected gets loose in here, we could all be lost. We'll have to find another way," he stated, opening the door to the refrigeration unit.

After tossing Alexa a bag of A-negative, he grabbed one for himself and sank down to the floor as he drank. "Will you be able to help Layla, too?" he whispered.

Alexa, already feeling much stronger, pulled the nearly-empty blood bag from her lips. She licked a drop of stray blood from the corner of her mouth before responding. "I'm sorry, Dante. Ethan and I are bonded. From what I saw in Chloe's vision, that's how I can save him. But Claesson has had a team working nonstop to find a cure, so don't give up hope."

Dante sighed and crumpled the empty plastic in his fist. "Our people have been trying to find a cure for that fucking virus for centuries. It's stupid to think they're going to suddenly figure it out now."

Alexa didn't know what else to say; she knew he was right, but she still had hope. After everything she'd been through and seen, she couldn't help but believe in miracles.

CHAPTER 2 - *Picking Up the Pieces*

"I need an estimate on the number of casualties now," Commander Claesson barked into the phone while High Commander William Ryan and several Elite soldiers waited around the table in the pit. "Yeah, I got it. How many of those were human? And how many missing still unaccounted for? Okay, you call me back on this line the instant you know anything else or if anything else happens. No, cell communications are going to remain blacked out for now so it's landline communication only."

The Commander dropped into his chair and rubbed his temples. It had been hours since Chloe knocked him and his men out with a powerful mind blast, but he still felt a little off.

"Right now we're looking at thirty-two humans confirmed dead, fifteen still missing, plus eight civilian vampires dead and another twenty-four still unaccounted for. Unless we find bodies soon, it's pretty safe to assume that those civilians will be joining Lucias's ranks before the day's done."

"God, that's no doubt what the missing humans were taken for, to feed the newly- infected," Jester added, looking up from the screen of his laptop. He'd been glued to it for what seemed like forever; monitoring the news and communications in and around the city with the help of some civilian consultants and a couple Elite on other compounds, who'd remained behind to keep things running when the residents headed to Boston to join in the fight.

"So what does this mean for us?" Cami chimed in. With Layla's arrival and Dante's subsequent meltdown, she was the ranking officer on the compound under Commander Claesson. It had taken some persuading for Claesson to let her to step into the role considering how close she was to the recent events, but he'd given in under the condition that Jackson shadowed her so he could take over in the event things became too personal for her.

Commander Claesson shifted his focus to William, looking for some guidance on the rather uncertain subject. "As of right now, we're going to maintain the physical lockdown of the compound; no one in or out without my or Commander Claesson's express permission," the High Commander stated.

"The remainder of our Elite reinforcements should be arriving within the next twenty-four hours, and Esther will be here with some other witches from the Boston coven to cast more protective spells over the compound as soon as the sun comes up and ensures that Lucias's men won't be a threat," Claesson added.

"Am I to understand that we will not be sending a team out to search for Chloe?" Cami asked careful to keep her tone neutral.

"I'm afraid that is the case. My granddaughter chose to leave with Lucias for a reason. I'm not sure what that reason was yet, but either way, according to the Commander's assessments, we're not in a position to make a stand against Lucias yet. Going after Chloe, without sufficient resources, puts her at even greater risk. Lucias will sacrifice every man he has in order to keep her and he has a lot more men than we do right now."

As hard as it was to sit on her hands while her niece was carted off by their greatest enemy, the man responsible for so many terrible crimes against their people and her family in particular, she knew the High Commander was right.

"So what do you want us to tell the rest of our people?" Jackson asked.

"The truth," Commander Claesson replied without hesitation. "As much as we can, at least, since there's no hiding what happened here tonight. With the communications blackout, I'm not too worried about information leaking to the civilian population and I think we're beyond the point of keeping this shit a secret. Our people need to start preparing themselves; Elite and civilian. The battle is coming, and it appears it will be sooner rather than later. Most Boston personnel already know that Layla was abducted. Let them know Lucias used her to breach our outer defenses and Chloe drew them off before they made it inside, allowing us to recover Layla who will be remaining in quarantine for the time being. That's all we know."

"And then what?" Cami pressed.

"When Boston personnel are up to speed, I want you to meet with the ranking officers from the other compounds who are onsite and fill them in as well. Let them handle telling their own people."

"There are going to be a lot of questions," Cami replied, shifting in her seat uneasily.

"Then we'll keep the men focused on their duties instead of standing around gossiping. We need all of our resources working together to get the new soldiers settled in, and I want everyone divided into groups running training drills around the clock. Work with the other officers to determine tactical teams. Research has developed some new rounds," Claesson said pulling a bullet from his pocket, "the tips are filled with silver nitrate," he continued, shaking it to show the shimmery liquid. "Our solid silver rounds keep the infected from healing, but those can easily be removed. With these, the silver enters the bloodstream so our targets get a lot bigger. Hitting them anywhere is damn near as good as a shot to the head."

Claesson tossed the round in the air and Cami easily grabbed it. She smiled as she spun it between her fingers. "We've got three thousand rounds ready to go. After everyone's up to speed and divided up, get them distributed."

Cami nodded her understanding. "Okay, you know what to do, get to it," Claesson said, dismissing the group. "Jester, we need you to hang back," he added, grabbing the young vampire's shoulder before he made it to the door.

Commander Claesson gestured to the closest chair, encouraging Jester to sit. The High Commander followed suit, pulling his seat up to him while Claesson remained standing.

"I wanted to speak with you privately for a few moments, Jester," William began. "Commander Claesson and I have discussed it, but before I take it to the rest of the Agency, I wanted to get your input on the human integration protocols. You've shown yourself to be well-versed in the current technologies and human culture and, while I'm confident in our experts, I'd like a fresh pair of eyes to take a look. Once it's done, it cannot be undone and the future of our race depends on its success."

The High Commander placed a thick folder labeled 'Confidential: Agency Eyes Only' on the table. "It goes without saying that you are not to breathe a word of this to anyone else, under any circumstances. I fear we'll have to make an announcement soon enough, but until then the utmost secrecy is vital."

"Of course, my lord," Jester replied, feeling honored by the level of trust being placed in him by one of the most powerful and important vampires in the world.

"Is everything all set up?" William asked, looking at his reflection in the glass while he adjusted his lavender tie and smoothed the collar of his charcoal shirt.

"Yes, my lord," Jester replied as William slipped his black suit jacket up his arms. "I've swept the room for transmitters again and implemented a temporary lockdown of the corridor so we will have complete privacy for the videoconference, as requested. All of the attendants have responded and will be joining in on time."

"Excellent. Thank you, Jester. I appreciate all of your hard work on this. With all you've done on this, in addition to your other duties on the compound, I know you can't have gotten any sleep over the last two days. Why don't you go get some rest?"

"If it's all the same to you, my lord, I'd like to stay just in case you run into any technical problems with the connection equipment or the presentation material I prepared."

"Of course; if you feel up to it. Thank you for your dedication," William replied.

"I'll agree to that, on one condition," Commander Claesson interjected. "You can stay if you feed; we've got about ten minutes yet," he said, tossing a bag of blood over the table to Jester's waiting hands. "You're pale enough to make some of the myths about us seem true," he teased.

"Thank you, sir," Jester replied gratefully before tearing through the bag with his fangs. Despite the Commander's constant comments over the week, he had, in fact, forgotten to feed.

"You know, Alek, I'm beginning to think our suspicions of a traitor may have been misguided," William said as Jester started on a second bag of blood and they waited for the meeting to begin. "I've been diligent in my, let's call them, investigations," he said, tapping his temple. "I've spoken to all personnel who possess a high level of clearance and I've listened in on everyone else I've come in contact with. So far there hasn't been anything that would indicate treason."

"Perhaps, but it's still not worth the risk; and if everything goes as planned we'll find out soon enough. I hate to think of what would happen if Lucias gets wind of our plans before we get everything in place," Commander Claesson replied.

"Yes; we're only going to get one shot at this so we have to be certain we don't tip our hand too soon. Even with the element of surprise, we remain at a disadvantage against Lucias's army of infected."

"My lord, it's time," Jester said as images of Agency members and other leaders from around the world began popping up on the screen.

"Good morning, friends," William began, immediately switching into High Commander mode. "Thank you for joining us. I warn you in advance, this is going to be a long process so please try to be patient. After all, we're only about to change the course of history."

CHAPTER 3 - *New Friends*

"I've been patient with her, but I will not wait much longer," Lucias stated as he paced across his office. "You assured me with your last vision that she will come around on her own," he continued, pointing at Asana who sat nervously in front of his desk. She was used to Lucias's temper and impatience; being so valuable to him had always kept her safe, but now that he was so close to obtaining so much power, she was afraid. Afraid for herself, and for Anna, the daughter Lucias had been holding prisoner for many years. He used Anna to ensure Asana's complete cooperation since he could not infect her with his virus. Shortly after its development, Lucias captured and infected a vampire who could manipulate fire. Once his transformation was complete, the ability completely disappeared, rendering him no more useful than any other infected vampire in the army.

"I cannot control my visions, Sire, but I have seen her standing with you in battle against The Elite with a great army under your command; an army far larger than the one you currently possess and I sense that she is content. Beyond that, I cannot yet see, but despite her power, she is a gentle soul and so very young. It would be unwise to push her. "

"Yes, perhaps you are right," Lucias conceded, satisfied with the expectation of gaining Chloe's allegiance; for the time being. He visited her daily, doing all he could to control his baser urges in her presence. While in truth, her innocence and gentility turned him off, he craved the power the mate bond would give him over her. He felt himself growing hard just thinking of dominating such a woman as Chloe. Though he would never admit it to anyone, he was actually afraid of her, which made her all the more enticing to a man like him.

"Return to your quarters and continue your work. I want you focused on her future night and day, and you are to alert me the moment you see anything new," Lucias commanded before exiting the office, intent on finding some release.

Molly was always close by and had proven quite useful in helping him remain restrained with Chloe. Unfortunately, though she should have known better than to question him, she was growing increasingly bold and constantly inquired about his intentions to turn her into a vampire. It wasn't that he didn't want to. In his way, he almost loved her, but despite the notions of popular fiction, turning a human into one of his kind was impossible. He could have forced her to obey him, like so many others who came before her, but somehow she was different; he craved her twisted affection like a drug and he suspected that, once she knew she was destined to live out her life as a human, the spell would be broken.

"No matter," Lucias mumbled to himself as he made his way to the playroom, where he often enjoyed the rough pleasure of Molly's company. He would make use of her for as long as she continued to please him, and when she didn't, he would simply dispose of her.

Kaleb lay on his bed, the door to his quarters left slightly ajar as he remained completely still with his eyes closed, barely breathing as he listened. Since Chloe's arrival, he'd done little beyond that; only getting up to eat or, when he was certain his father was sufficiently occupied, sit in the corridor just beyond Chloe's quarters. He wouldn't even have bothered much with eating if he wasn't so concerned about keeping up his strength, but he knew what he was going to have to do. He would have to find a way to kill his father, because there was no way he was going to let such a foul man touch the beautiful creature who'd stolen his heart with a single glance.

His lips turned up just slightly at the thought of her.

You should get some sleep.

He heard her sweet voice whisper in his mind.

I need to protect you. He sent back with determination.

He's not going to hurt me, but he'll kill you, or worse, if you give him a reason. Don't worry about me. Chloe replied.

How can you know; have you seen it with certainty? Do you know what will happen? Kaleb asked. Chloe's silence told him she didn't know.

He hadn't seen or physically spoken to Chloe since the day his father took her from The Elite compound, yet he felt closer to her than he'd been to another person since before his brother died. It was such a strange and unsettling thing at first, hearing another voice in his head, but he'd known it was her immediately.

Concerned that he'd pushed her too far, Kaleb tried to change the subject. *I wonder if you really sound the way you do in my head. I was so entranced the first time I saw you, I'm not sure I ever heard you speak.*

It's been my experience that people sound exactly the same in their own minds as they do when they speak, so I'm guessing this is how you will hear me when we're finally together.

Kaleb's heart began to pound at the thought. He'd never wanted anything more in his long life. His mind raced with images of his fingers stroking her cheek, his lips pressed to hers and he suddenly found it hard to catch his breath.

You're making me blush, Chloe sent with a giggle.

I'm sorry, Kaleb replied, sitting up and opening his eyes.

Please, don't apologize, I was only teasing. You know, I like it when you think about me that way.

25

She did love it. She loved him and she knew he loved her, even if they'd never actually talked to or touched one another. They'd spent the better part of the past week exploring each other's minds, or at least, she had explored his and told him what was in hers. There was an openness in him that surprised her. He never tried to block her from his thoughts, even those which were most dark, so she literally knew everything there was to know about him.

I have to go, we'll talk later. And don't worry, it's not him. Chloe sent and was gone.

Kaleb found himself completely alone again. He strained to hear across the building to Chloe's quarters, but was only met with the residual noise of the building.

It must be Asana, he thought, feeling grateful to Chloe for reassuring him that it wasn't his father who was disrupting her. He spent all of his time worrying about what that evil man might do before he had the chance to stop him. Lucias visited Chloe every day, and every day Kaleb sat poised, his body drawn like a bowstring ready to let loose at the slighted indication of distress from Chloe. Though, what would he really be able to do? His father was older and stronger, not to mention that he had the advantage of control through the sire bond. One resonant command and he could put Kaleb on his knees. No, Kaleb knew that when the time came, he would have to act quickly and strike before his father knew he was coming.

Lucias was an evil man, there was no doubting that, but still somehow, Kaleb struggled with the thought of patricide. Lucias was the only family he had in the world. Though he loved Chloe, in his heart, he knew her family would never give their blessing to a union with a man such as him. Especially her father. Still, he dared to hope.

He's growing impatient. I don't know how much longer I can hold him at bay. Asana sent sitting cross-legged on the floor pretending to meditate. Chloe, are you there?

It was several moments before Chloe finally responded.

Yes, I'm here.

You were talking to him again weren't you? You must be careful with him, he is his father's son. It could be a trick.

No, Asana, you're wrong about him. He is nothing like Lucias. He's kind and sweet and yes, I realize how ridiculously crazy it is, but I love him.

I won't question your judgment, as your abilities are far beyond my own; perhaps you can see things that elude me, but I just want you to be careful. Do not reveal too much to him.

Don't worry about me; I know what I'm doing. Chloe replied. Before Asana could even ask, Chloe answered the question that was burning in her mind. I'm sorry, but I cannot see Anna either, even with the necklace.

Chloe looked down as she smoothed her fingers over the sterling silver locket. Asana had taken a great risk sneaking it to Chloe, in the hopes that having something that once belonged to her daughter would help focus her foresight.

It must be a spell. I have always had difficulty seeing anything about my own life no matter how hard I tried, but you are much stronger than any seer I have ever met. If you cannot find her, he has found a witch to block her from me, or it is as I have always feared.

Chloe didn't need to ask what she meant; the grief in Asana's next thought like a physical presence floating between them.

It had been decades since Lucias had allowed her to visit with her daughter, so long that she wondered if he had long ago had her killed. But it was too much of a risk to ask him. When Lucias first captured her she rebelled against him, refusing to use her ability to help him. That was until he abducted and imprisoned her only daughter as leverage. For many years he used threats against Anna to control her, then one day when he came to her there was no mention of Anna. Though it pained her, Asana did not ask about her daughter after that day, instead choosing to feign loyalty to the man she despised above all others, biding her time. Over the years, as she continued to give her visions freely, Lucias began to trust her more and more. Her prison was exchanged for a suite, her tattered rags for the finest of garments. He even allowed her some access to Chloe to aid with her visions, but only if he accompanied her, a privilege afforded to her alone. No one else was allowed to see or talk to Chloe, not even his own son or his favored pet Molly.

In those precious moments with Chloe, Asana found a kindred spirit, someone who could understand her in a way few others could. Like

Asana, Chloe was merely a tool to Lucias, a means to the end he desired so greatly. To Asana, Chloe was the only friend she'd had in over two centuries, and she was Chloe's only way out.

Chloe's ability to listen to and read thoughts provided a unique opportunity. Lucias had placed cameras and recording devices in Chloe's room, preventing Asana from speaking freely about her plans and visions. But that first day, when Asana stepped through the door, Chloe read her mind. Being the brilliant girl she was, Chloe let Asana know they could talk, really talk, without being heard, while appearing to be engaged in meaningless small talk. In that moment, Asana felt a sense of hope and relief that she hadn't known for two-hundred years. That first night, she shared her long struggle with Chloe, telling her about Anna and the terrible things Lucias forced her to help him do. They spoke of Chloe's family and how Asana had truly been trying to protect them all along, always holding back information whenever she could in order to give them time to escape.

It was impossible to hold her visions back entirely for, like Chloe's grandmother, Josephine, Asana's visions took a physical toll, often causing her to faint or even fall into a coma and Lucias was always watching. After learning all of that, Chloe began guiding Asana so that she could tap into her future stream, a feat which had even eluded her powerful grandmother, Josephine. In practicing her ability, Chloe had learned how to open her own future to the sight of others, so long as she removed the charmed necklace that still hung around her neck. In return, Asana swore to never reveal anything to Lucias that could hurt Chloe or the ones she loved.

Have you seen anything else? Asana inquired, wondering how close they were to the impending battle she'd foreseen.

Nothing of consequence, Chloe lied again. She had, in fact, had a vision of Anna. Lucias would bring her to the compound to punish Asana, for what Chloe could not see, nor could she see what transpired after. That was the way of her visions. Whenever a future involved a choice which could send it in more than one direction, Chloe's vision remained unfocused until events drew nearer or a definite choice was made. This particular choice seemed to belong to Asana.

CHAPTER 4 - *A Plan Comes Together*

"Jared, it's been a week already. Isn't there something Cami can do? He's her brother; won't they at least let *her* in to see him?" Alexa asked as she flopped down onto her brother's bed.

"Trust me, she's doing all she can, but she's swamped with her duties now and even Father agrees it's too great a risk until we know more about how the virus is affecting him. They are worried turning him and Layla over to us is a trick; that he's given them a secret command or something to attack the first chance they get," Jared replied, putting his hand on her shoulder.

"They are locked up behind impenetrable glass; what will it hurt to just let me see Ethan and Dante see Layla? Or at least tell Ethan I'm alive."

"Alexa, from what Cami managed to get out of the assistant working for one of the few doctors allowed access, Ethan hasn't spoken and he's barely moved since he got here. You have to prepare yourself; he might not even understand if they do tell him."

"And he might not recognize me when I do see him," she recited, having heard the same words spoken again and again by people trying to appease and console her. "None of that matters; I've told you and everyone else already, our bond will bring him back!" she yelled growing frustrated.

"You realize that's one of the main reasons they are reluctant to let you near him. What did you think would happen when you told them you want to let an infected vampire bite you? What if you're wrong, Alexa? You'll be infected and you'll put everyone in the compound at risk."

"Then they can lock me in there, too. At least then we'll be together, but I'm not wrong and you all know it," Alexa replied, feeling defeated. She'd shared Chloe's vision with her brother and father, both also telepaths, so they'd seen firsthand what needed to happen in order for Ethan to be saved.

Jared sighed. The bed dipped under his weight as he sat down beside her. "I do trust Chloe's visions, but you know how that works; the future is never set in stone. What she showed you was supposed to occur on the day she left, something could have changed; the virus may have taken a stronger hold. We all love you, sis; you have to understand the concern."

"Of course I do, Jared, but what would you do if it was Cami?" Alexa asked pointedly.

Without even realizing it, Jared was clenching his jaw tightly with his fists squeezing so tight his knuckles were white.

"Exactly." Alexa said correctly reading her brother's reaction. They both knew he would take on the world to save the woman he loved.

"Yeah, okay," Jared said as he started to relax again, "but what can we do? Dante told you that no one can get into that area without Commander Claesson, and it's not just some code we can pull from his thoughts. We're talking biometric security here; a retinal scan and full handprint, so unless you're suggesting we cut off his hand and pop out an eye, we're going to need to persuade him to let you in."

"Ugh, if only there was some way I could sneak in when he lets the doctor in. Fucking vampire senses; he'd know I was coming from a hundred yards away, if I could even get *that* close. The guards in the corridors won't let me past the training wing," Alexa said with exasperation as she flopped down onto the bed.

"What about when the doc comes back out? Does the Commander have to open the door?" Jared asked.

"I have no clue; like I said, I can't get anywhere near there. Why?" Alexa asked, her brows knitted together with confusion.

"I may have an idea, but we're going to need some serious help. Come on," Jared said jumping up and pulling her out the door.

"Shit, that could actually work," Cami said, her mouth turning up in an admiring half-smile as she looked up at Jared. "We'll need Dante; he's the only one who can talk Martinez into doing something so crazy, and Jasmine for the guard."

"Martinez did it to sneak me out on that mission to the human's farm house. How hard could it be to get him to help us now?" Jared asked somewhat sarcastically. They all knew this was a much more daunting task. Taking Jared off the compound during lockdown endangered Jared alone. Unauthorized access to infected prisoners put the whole compound, hell, maybe even the world, at risk.

"Getting Dante's help won't be a problem," Alexa added. "He wants to see Layla as badly as I want to see Ethan."

"Therein lays the problem," Cami added. "Chloe saw you saving my brother, not Layla. The mate bond is a powerful thing. Seeing you may be enough to keep him under control, but Layla and Dante aren't bonded; she's too unpredictable. I don't know if we can trust him in there with her."

"Are you suggesting we tell Dante that he has to hang back while someone else goes in? Yeah, good luck with that," Jared stated. Though Dante had been MIA most of the week since Cami had taken over his command, the few times Jared had caught a glimpse of him, Layla was the only thing on his mind and Cami had been witness to more than one shouting match between him and Commander Claesson about the same subject.

No, if anyone was going to get into that room, they weren't doing it without Dante.

"Fuck," Cami muttered, moving to the door. "Let's get this over with. Who knows how much time we have before Lucias makes his next move."

A loud clang reverberated through the training room as the defenseless training dummy slammed into a metal pole. Dante had taken a page from Cami's book, spending all the time he wasn't occupied with Elite business punishing his body and inanimate objects unfortunate enough to be within striking distance. Since he'd been relieved of command, he didn't have much Elite business to worry about anyway.

The soft squeak of the door opening raked across his nerves like nails on a chalkboard, since he assumed it was another idiot coming to spew the same old bullshit about how they would find a cure, that he needed to sleep, blah, blah, blah. What he needed was Layla and until he could have her, physical pain was the only thing that dulled the ache in his heart.

He didn't bother looking to see who it was, intent on continuing his workout in the hopes that the intruder would take the hint and leave, but he stopped as the familiar and comforting scent of Alexa hit his nose. She was the only person he could stand to be around because she was the only one who truly understood what he was going through.

Turning to face her, he opened his arms. Alexa walked into them without hesitation. The embrace served two purposes; it provided them both with some measure of comfort and it allowed Dante, as a mirror, to take on Alexa's ability temporarily. Unlike Chloe, Alexa couldn't speak into the mind of another who wasn't a telepath. Speaking directly into one another's minds came in quite handy, since most of what they discussed involved disobeying Commander Claesson's direct order to stay away from Ethan and Layla.

Before Cami and Jared had even stepped into the room, Alexa had telepathically relayed their entire plan to Dante. Unfortunately, because her mind was so open to him in that moment, he also knew of Cami's desire to keep him from going in with Alexa.

Dante glared at Cami pointedly, ignoring Jared who stepped between them protectively. Both men knew that Cami didn't need anyone's protection; she could take care of herself being one of if not *the* best fighter in The Elite, but Jared couldn't help himself. Sometimes his primal need to take care of the woman he loved, a woman who could easily kick his ass, overrode logic.

Cami didn't even get annoyed by Jared's display. She was starting to find his occasional macho display endearing rather than insulting.

"Don't worry about Martinez; he'll do it," Dante stated, still pinning Cami with his stare, "but you can take your concerns and shove them up your ass. I'm going, too."

"Don't fucking talk to her like that," Jared growled, taking a step towards the much larger vampire. Cami shot between them, stopping Jared before he picked a fight he couldn't win. While he and Dante were certainly on better terms than before, when they were essentially fighting over Cami, with what was going on with Layla, Dante was pretty much always in the mood for a fight. It didn't matter if it was against friend or foe.

She reached back and took Jared's fisted hand without taking her eyes from Dante, in case more intervention was necessary. Jared's hand relaxed in hers as she spoke, though she could still feel the tension in his body as he leaned into her back.

"Listen, Dante. I get it and it was stupid to think we could keep you out, but you have to understand why we're worried," Cami said, craning her neck to look into Dante's fierce eyes while standing in such close proximity. "You can't know how you'll feel when you see her locked up, so I need your word you won't open the door to her cell no matter what happens. We're going in there so Alexa can cure Ethan. If that works, it will be proof that curing the infection is possible and it might give the scientists a new angle to work from. Then the Commander might be more reasonable about letting you visit Layla."

"She's right, Dante," Alexa said, softly placing her hand on his arm. The simple touch seemed to dissipate some of the aggression from the air around him.

"You have my word. I'm not going to try and free Layla; I just need to see her," Dante said, his tone softening as he thought of seeing Layla's beautiful face again.

Ethan sat on the cold floor of his cell with his back against the wall.

He only moved from his position there to retrieve the bags of blood the scientists shoved to him through the tray securely inserted into the impenetrable plexi-glass of his cell. Of course, he had to pay a price for them.

"We need another sample." Ethan heard in an artificial sounding voice, as the researcher on duty pressed the button that provided the only source of outside sound into the plastic cage.

In a flash so fast it was almost difficult for the waiting vampire to track, Ethan moved to stand before the man who jumped back several inches, unable to hide his fear despite the several inches of unbreakable barrier that stood between him and the infected vampire they all feared.

With the touch of another button, a small round piece of the glass slid over. Having been subjected to the process several times a day for the past week, Ethan slid his arm into the slot, never taking his glowing red eyes off the throat of the other vampire. His fangs descended to their full length as he watched the steady strum of the scientist's abnormally rapid pulse. A part of him was excited by the man's fear and he inhaled deeply to take in the scent of the emotion, which seeped through the small opening, before a silver cuff clamped down on his arm, locking it in place.

Ethan didn't even flinch as the cold metal burned into his flesh; the pain was nothing, he was nothing. He had lost everything. A wife destroyed by his own hand. A daughter stolen by the one he hated most in the world, but was bound by blood to serve until his last breath.

The nervous vampire made quick work of drawing the required sample of blood. The opening closed from the outside and Ethan's arm was released. He collected his offered reward from the tray and made quick work of the three bags of red liquid. The beast inside him paced, anxious and dissatisfied. It wanted to hunt. It wanted fresh blood; to feel the beat of its victim's heart as he drained every drop of blood.

But as quickly as the monster started to rise, a calming presence enveloped his mind and overwhelming grief gripped what was left of his heart.

Alexa. he thought, sinking back into his normal spot. He continued to feel her as strongly as ever, and though he knew it was only in his mind, she was the only thing that allowed him to hold on to the tiny shred that remained of who he once was. At the same time, feeling her in that way was the worst form of torture. He often wished it would stop, that he could just give in to the beast and his bloodlust and never look back, but he'd promised to hold on as long as he could for her, because it is what she would want.

There came a point with all infected when, while they resembled who they once were and were basically in control, they no longer had any humanity. No remorse. No love. They followed orders without question and they took what they wanted from whoever was unlucky enough to stumble across their path and never looked back. For most, it occurred as part of the initial transformation; but for Ethan, it was different.

As had become the normal progression of his silent torture, his thoughts turned to Chloe, and the scene of her giving herself over to Lucias replayed in his mind. For the briefest of moments he tried to convince himself that he will rescue her, hoping in some way that it will give him redemption for his sins against Alexa, but his beast's low guttural laugh mocks him. He was powerless to act against his master, so he would remain just as he was; a feral animal in the cage it deserved.

After seeing the pain his friend had been in for the past week, and knowing how powerful Chloe was, as Dante suspected it didn't take much persuading to get Martinez to agree to help them, and Layla was Jasmine's best friend, so she was in without any hesitation.

He stood completely still; concentrating on the impenetrable mist he was casting over himself, Dante, and Alexa as they waited for Jared's signal.

With Cami still being allowed access to all areas of the compound, except the lab where Ethan and Layla were being held, it was easy enough sneaking the veiled trio to within a few yards of the final door they needed to pass through. For two days after devising their entry plan, Cami had been watching the Commander and the scientists who were allowed access to Ethan and Layla, carefully noting the amount of time that passed between Claesson opening the outer door and the scientist exiting, which they were able to do simply using the general access code for most doors to the compound. This was a lucky piece of information Alexa was able to pluck from one of the unsuspecting vampire's minds when he wasn't making much of an effort to keep up his mental shields.

"I'm so nervous," Alexa whispered, so quietly that Dante wouldn't have been able to hear if he weren't a vampire.

"You don't have to whisper, Alexa. Martinez's mojo blocks the sound, too," Dante said, feeling rather anxious himself, more from the thought of seeing Layla rather than the worry of being caught. As far as he was concerned, there wasn't much the Commander could do to him that was worse than what he was living through already.

"I know; it just feels weird talking with the guard so close," Alexa said a little more loudly, as she continued to watch the guard talking to Cami and Jared.

Cami had concocted a reason to enter the corridor so they could chat with the guard and distract him while the others snuck in. There was a soldier tasked with delivering blood to the various guards posted around the compound and, while he'd been making his rounds near the residential wing, Jasmine lured him into her quarters where Cami hit him with a powerful sedative dart. Cami hated involving anyone else, but she couldn't very well risk discovery by shooting the unsuspecting vampire in the corridor, which was in plain view of the security cameras. The soldier was visiting from another compound and eager to impress the Commander, so there was no way he would deviate from his duties without a little help from Jasmine, whose talent was in persuasion. A little memory manipulation and the soldier would be convinced he'd spent the missing time thoroughly enjoying the pleasure of Jasmine's company and, since he would have had to abandon his duties in order to do so, his silence was all but assured.

With the original courier securely restrained in Jasmine's bathroom, Cami took his delivery and met Jared before heading to the containment unit. The guard didn't bat an eye when she explained that the regular courier had been called away for a special training session in preparation for an imminent attack on the compound. With everything that had happened over the past few weeks, the fear of attack hung heavy in the air of every vampire community, including the compound.

After what seemed like forever to Alexa, Jared finally gave the signal, placing his hand on Cami's right shoulder.

"Did you hear that?" Cami asked, interrupting the guard's explanation of the security protocols from his compound and looking off to the left away from her and Jared.

"I didn't hear anything," the guard replied, taking a step towards Cami while focusing his preternatural hearing down the corridor.

When the door to the containment unit slid open, the guard startled, and they all laughed a little as the exiting scientist shuffled away without acknowledging any of them, keeping his eyes focused intently on the notes he was making on his tablet.

"I guess it was just my imagination," Cami said, turning back towards the door to the containment unit as it slid closed. Her eyes darted around, looking for the telltale, though nearly imperceptible, shimmer of Martinez's mist. With the guard being from another compound, he would never have seen Martinez's ability so, even if he noticed the anomaly, it wouldn't register as anything other than warm air moving around. When she found no sign of it, she knew her friends had made it through the door in time.

"I think we've kept you from your duties long enough, soldier," Cami said, taking Jared's hand. "I'd love to hear more about those new security procedures later."

With that, she and Jared disappeared around the corner.

✧

"Now we wait," Cami said as soon as the soundproofing to her quarters engaged.

"I'm starting to feel like this was a bad idea," Jared said, running a hand through his already tousled locks. Cami's eyes followed the motion. She loved the way it made his sandy hair looked like he'd just gotten out of bed. "No one will be entering that room for almost an hour. What if something goes wrong? I should have gone with them," he continued, oblivious to her stare.

"Dante and Martinez will protect Alexa. We have to trust that Chloe's vision was correct," Cami replied, pulling Jared down to the bed. "I can't believe I'm saying this, but now that I have you, now that I know what true love is like, I know their bond is strong enough to save my brother."

She took Jared's face in her hands and stared into his eyes for several long seconds, the lust that had just started to simmer in hers giving way to something deeper. The love that flowed between them seemed to fill the surrounding air, blocking out everything else. Their lips drifted closer and closer, drawn to one another like magnets until they finally came together. The kiss was soft and sweet, full of nurturing and comfort.

"There's nothing we can do for now," Cami whispered, drawing back slightly, her lips drifting over his as she spoke. "I don't want to waste this time together."

The future was so uncertain. They both knew the world could be turned upside down at any moment; right now was the only time that was guaranteed.

When their mouths met again, there was urgency and desperation in their kiss. It was as if they were both pouring everything they had to give, every hope, every fear, into that one act.

Jared slipped his hands into Cami's soft curls, tugging her head back slightly to gain full access to her mouth. He swept his deft tongue across her swollen lips, then took the lower one between his teeth and tugged. He released it and groaned when Cami's fangs dropped from her gums, an undeniable indication of her desire. As if on cue, the scent of her arousal reached him and his own fangs lowered in response.

In a flash of movement, Jared had her pinned beneath him on the bed, his fingers making quick work of the buckles and snaps of her weapons harness. In their short time together, he'd become an expert in removing the many layers of her soldier's attire.

Cami pushed up to aid him in slipping the black leather over her shoulders and off her arms. When he pushed the contraption aside and it slid off the bed, the loud clang of her swords hitting the floor didn't faze either of them.

Unlike Jared, Cami didn't have the patience to undo all of the buttons holding his blue button-down shirt in place. She simple grabbed each side of his shirt and yanked, sending white buttons flying in all directions.

Jared flashed a lopsided grin; her impatience thrilled him. She was the most passionate and uninhibited woman he'd ever known; something he would never have guessed when they first met. He continued to hover over her, just looking down, taking in her remarkable beauty despite the insistent throb in his strained jeans.

Not in the mood to take it slowly, Cami grabbed Jared's shoulder and had him on his back before he could protest. Once in control, her favorite place to be, she had the rest of their clothes on the floor before the next beat of their vampire hearts.

As much as she wanted to feel him inside her, Cami couldn't help but pause to take in the masculine beauty of the man she could now freely admit she loved. Her eyes drifted from his full lips turned up in that sexy grin he often wore, to the golden skin covering his pecs and chiseled abs. A shiver went through her when her gaze reached the light trail of dark blonde hair, most of which was covered by his thick length laying slightly to the side and almost reaching his navel.

She licked her lips, considering how the soft, skin-covered hard steel would feel and taste in her mouth. Jared's cock jumped, her thought flowing freely to him. She normally didn't like for him to listen in on her thoughts, but the couple had quickly discovered it was an amazing ability to have when it came to making love.

She glanced to up at Jared and he tilted his head, his expression asking "what are you waiting for?"

Cami didn't need any more encouragement. She slid back on the bed and grabbed the base of Jared's cock in her hand. She put the head against her mouth, and then slowly smeared the drop of clear liquid rising from the tip over her lips. Jared growled low when she started to slide her lips over the head, moving achingly slowly towards the base as she flicked her tongue skillfully over the underside of his shaft. She took him in as far as she could, using her fist to cover the inches her lips couldn't reach, before she moved back up, going just as slowly.

Jared's body was trembling with the need to move as Cami continued her delicious torture, stroke after unhurried stroke, until he didn't think he could take anymore.

"Fuck, Cami. Please," he muttered grabbing her shoulders, wanting her to stop and to keep going at the same time.

She finally released him with a triumphant smile. He started to rise, wanting to take control, but Cami planted a firm palm on his chest and pushed him back to the bed.

"I didn't say you could get up yet," she said, sliding her hips forward, covering the length of his cock with her wetness before she reach between them and positioned his length at her opening. She hovered there, moving up and down so slightly, testing him, teasing him, until he grabbed her hips and forced her down, filling her in one motion.

Cami cried out as he stretched her to the limit, at the razor's edge of pain and pleasure. He kept his grip tight on her hips and rocked her back and forth, knowing from her thoughts how much she loved the way his length pushed against her most sensitive of places when he was buried so deep. He released one of her hips and used his thumb to rub her swollen clit as she took over rocking against him.

The warm fire of her orgasm flooded over her and she instinctually turned her head and sunk her fangs into Jared's wrist, unable to resist the extra burst his blood would give her climax.

Jared moaned as her teeth pierced his skin and the walls of her pussy clenched around his hardness and moisture dripped down the base and onto his heavy sac.

Without waiting for her orgasm to end, Jared pulled his wrist away from her mouth and flipped Cami to her back. He buried his face in the crook of her neck and inhaled as he thrust hard. His mouth felt full with his fully extended fangs as her sweet essence called to him. Cami pulled his head closer, urging him on, wanting to feel the delicious sting of his bite as much as he wanted to taste her blood. When he struck, she immediately cried out his name as another orgasm claimed her. With her blood sliding down his throat, his release was quick to follow, his cock throbbing in sync with her pulse against his lips.

When the last wave of his climax had passed, Jared released Cami's neck and slid his tongue over the two punctures to speed the healing. She followed suit, pulling his wrist to her mouth as he collapsed on the bed beside her.

Jared pulled her into his arms and she nestled her ass against him, his cock still hard against her as he kissed the back of her neck.

"I love you, Camille," he whispered against her ear. She normally hated being called that, which is why no one ever did, but that somehow made it special when Jared used her full name.

"I love you, too," she replied with a sigh as she started to move away.

"Please don't get up yet," Jared pleaded.

"Five minutes," she conceded, knowing all hell was about to break loose on the compound whether she stayed or went. Even if everything went exactly as they hoped and Ethan was cured, there would likely be consequences for her and the other soldiers who'd disobeyed the Commander, a fact she conveniently neglected to share with Jared. Martinez was the only one who could have snuck past the guard; Claesson would know that, so she and Dante had devised a plan to exonerate him, but that would implicate Dante. Jasmine's role was far enough removed that she didn't have to worry, but Claesson was ancient and smart; he would figure out they had more help. A quick review of the security footage would point to Cami and if it didn't, there was the chance Rachel would be pissed off enough to turn her in.

As if on cue, a soft groan came from the bathroom, letting them know their time was up.

"She is going to be so pissed," Jared said before placing one last kiss on Cami's cheek and quickly dressing.

"Yeah, I'm guessing Martinez is going to have some choice words for us as well," Cami replied, following suit.

CHAPTER 5 - *Saving Ethan*

Alexa took a deep breath, trying to slow the pounding of her heart as she leaned against Dante just inside the door to the containment unit. But the spike in her anxiety wasn't due to her fear. It was Ethan. Her body was responding to their bond and it was clear to her that he felt her closeness as strongly as she felt his. She wondered what he must be thinking. Did he feel her and believe she was alive, or did his mind, altered by the virus, make him believe it was something more sinister, perhaps even a trick perpetrated by his evil master?

"Are you all right?" Dante asked with concern, as his well-trained eyes scanned the area around them. There was one security camera covering the corridor they were in, and two in the room where Ethan and Layla were being held. They could easily avoid the first by remaining within Martinez's mist until they entered the other room. Once inside, Dante would have to work quickly to disable the other two; one was pointed directly at Ethan, and the other covered Layla's cell and the lab where the scientists worked with the samples they took from Layla and Ethan. The point of taking out the cameras wasn't to cover their tracks, as it was inevitable that at least some of them would be caught, but to buy them time for Alexa to get to Ethan. The security feeds around the compound were constantly monitored; if they were seen in the restricted area, a full-scale lockdown could be initiated, making it impossible to open Ethan's cell.

"Yes, it's just Ethan; there's so much pain, I, I don't know how to describe how it feels," she said breathlessly gripping her chest.

"Alexa, you have to try to block him," Dante said, his brows furrowed with worry as Alexa shook in his arms.

Alexa took another deep breath and focused on Ethan and the invisible link between them, carefully pushing her mental shields against it without blocking the tie entirely because she feared what that would do to Ethan.

Dante immediately felt the change in her and loosened his hold. He steered Martinez, who was so deeply focused on maintaining the veil around them that he was completely oblivious to the conversation occurring right beside him, to the door. With the mist blocking the camera's view of the keypad, Dante entered the code that opened the door and they slipped inside.

Ethan's eyes snapped open and he scanned the empty room outside his cell. He knew there was only Layla there with him in the next cell, though he couldn't see her due to the wall that separated them. He gripped at his chest, trying to ease the ache that had overtaken him. It felt as if his heart was being tugged against his ribs. The beast within him grew restless and he could feel it pacing on the edge of his consciousness.

For the first time since he arrived, Ethan stood and moved towards the edge of his cage for something other than blood. He didn't understand why, but he needed to get up. The thick plexi-glass of his cell blocked all sounds and smells, but something was coming; he could feel it. A darkness covered his mind when he realized it was the blood bond. So it was as he had suspected all along. Lucias had been using the bond to torment him and he was certain his master was near. Perhaps he and his army of infected had invaded the compound and he was coming to retrieve his prized weapon.

While Ethan began to slip into despair as the last sliver of hope he had left faded away, his beast began to rise, eager to be unleashed by its master.

The red glow of his eyes reflected back at him from the glass, growing brighter and brighter until the door outside slid open.

Both parts of him waited anxiously, Ethan and his beast; one hungry for a fight, the other ready to give up. But no one appeared and the door closed again. As quickly as it rose, the pull from the bond lessened and Ethan began to calm. Was he losing what was left of his mind?

Alexa couldn't breathe. Tears flowed freely down her cheeks as she stared at the man she loved, seeing him for what felt like the very first time. To the man beside her, Ethan looked like some kind of demonic monster with his red eyes glowing bright, reflecting off of the glass before him and casting a red haze over his face, but she felt a peace she had not known since Eleuthera.

She started to move towards him, but Dante grabbed her; holding on tight as she fought against him.

"Alexa, wait! I have to get to the camera. If you step out there now, we'll be discovered and you won't have time to save him," he said aloud and into her mind for emphasis as he channeled her telepathy.

"I'm sorry," Alexa began, never taking her eyes off of Ethan. The glow in his eyes was fading and he turned away from her. "Please hurry, Dante."

In a flash, they were beneath the first camera where Dante made quick work of inserting the looping program he'd convinced Jester was needed for a recon mission in the city. Per Jester's instructions, it would need twenty seconds to record the feed to loop. In the meantime, Dante moved them to camera on the other side of the room and repeated the process.

"This is the longest twenty seconds of my life," Alexa stated, eager to finally reveal herself to Ethan.

Dante looked at the watch he'd strapped on specifically for this mission as the last few seconds ticked away. It was all he could do to keep his eyes on the digital screen. He'd vowed to not as much as look at Layla until he had Alexa safely in the room and Martinez could keep an eye on her and Ethan. Of course, he couldn't admit it to Cami, but she had been right to worry about him. He didn't exactly know what he was going to do when he finally saw Layla, but he was fairly certain, based on the scenarios that had been running through his head, that Cami wouldn't like it.

Ethan moved, intent on returning to his solitary space on the cold floor and the silent torture of his own mind until a flash of movement caught his eye.

He turned towards the source of motion, immediately falling to his knees as he took in Alexa's beautiful form standing a few short feet away.

I'm dreaming. He thought, never blinking or taking his eyes from her face. But he didn't recall allowing himself to sleep. Since becoming infected, he'd needed very little sleep and avoided it as much as possible because when he did dream, it was always the same nightmare. It was never anything as beautiful as what was before his eyes now. Perhaps, over the weeks, his memory of her had faded. Standing on the outside of his cell, she looked different somehow; more beautiful than he remembered if that was even possible.

Am I dead? he thought, hopeful that that was the case and this wasn't the start of a new nightmare or some sort of deception perpetrated by Lucias.

Despite the tears streaming down her face, Alexa smiled. Seeing the confusion and disbelief on Ethan's face and hearing the darkness of his thoughts, she placed her hand against her heart and dropped the mental shields she had in place to lessen the effects of their bond. She focused on all the love and joy she was feeling in that moment. The emotion was so powerful as it flowed between them, that Ethan's pain disappeared and his beast cowered in a dark corner of his mind.

For the first time since he transitioned, Ethan cried.

How can this be? Before the thought fully passed through his mind, he saw evidence of the change in Alexa as she moved with vampire speed to the panel which controlled the door to his cell.

Before he knew what was happening, the glass shifted. Alexa's scent filled his nostrils. His happiness at knowing she lived hadn't fully formed when the beast again reared its ugly head and a hunger overwhelmed him unlike any he'd known since he was first infected. He craved Alexa's blood so much it hurt. Panic flooded over him as he struggled for control.

Oh God, not again!

He bolted away, pushing himself back against the furthest corner of his cage. The small enclosure couldn't possible provide enough distance to lessen the effect her scent had on him, but he had to try. Despite his growing bloodlust and the pain that accompanied it, one undeniable thought reverberated in his mind. He couldn't go through it again. He wouldn't survive losing her twice.

Then something gave him a sliver of hope. In his fight for control, his eyes moved from Alexa and he saw for the first time that they were not alone. He needed to satisfy his bloodlust to regain control and he could do that with the blood of one of the males standing behind her.

Hearing the direction of his thoughts, Alexa stepped through the door, blocking Ethan's path to Martinez and Dante.

"Close it," she whispered, her voice strained by the shared pain of Ethan's bloodlust flowing through their connection. As they had planned, Martinez closed the door to Ethan's cell. Whatever happened next, Alexa's fate was tied to Ethan's.

Ethan's chest tightened at hearing her soft voice again, the sound lessening his pain for the briefest of moments before the need for blood again overtook him.

"Alexa, get out! Please don't do this again!" he tried to yell through clenched teeth, his gritty voice sounding strange to his own ears. It had been weeks since he'd heard its sound. His eyes glowing bright with bloodlust cast a red light on the floor as he kept his gaze trained downwards. He huddled in the corner, trembling as he fought an impossible battle.

"Ethan, please trust me. I will never leave you again. You need blood, my blood," Alexa whispered as she stepped closer. "I am stronger now; you can sense it, can't you? If you hurt me, I will heal. But you won't hurt me, I know you won't," she continued, lowering to her knees right in front him.

Ethan's body stilled and he slowly looked up as Alexa bared her fangs and bit into her own wrist, presenting it to him.

There was no fight left in him with the delicious aroma of her essence floating in the air, its source only inches away. Ethan took what was offered, gripping Alexa's arm with both hands as he drank. The first swallow of her blood was like pure heaven, and a warmth unlike anything he had ever felt before spread through his body, satisfying his bloodlust and calming the beast within.

He closed his eyes and swallowed again as Alexa leaned closer, stroking the side of his neck with her free hand and Ethan practically purred. She ran her tongue up the length of his carotid, calling it forward. Her bite was soft, gentle as she slid her fangs into his flesh and closed her eyes, relishing the first taste of his blood.

Surprised when Ethan released her wrist, Alexa moved away from his neck and lifted her lids to find the beautiful and familiar green-gray eyes of her husband staring back at her.

Dante had remained just below the security camera when Martinez lifted his concealing mist. As promised, he waited there until Alexa entered Ethan's cell and Martinez locked her in.

Finally, he let his eyes go to Layla's cell and all the air rushed from his lungs as tears welled up in his eyes. She was standing at the edge of the glass staring directly at him, her eyes shining red and her golden blonde hair cascading over her shoulders. She smiled, revealing fully-extended fangs as she crooked her finger at Dante, beckoning him to her.

"Dante man, watch yourself with her," Martinez cautioned from his position at the control panel. Layla might look like herself for the most part, but he'd had enough experience with the infected over the years to know she was anything but. She was a slave to Lucias and her own desires and she'd do whatever she could to get what she wanted, including hurting the man she'd once loved.

Martinez ran his fingers over the syringe in his pocket, praying it wouldn't come to that, but before they'd come down, Alexa had warned him that Dante wasn't quite thinking clearly when it came to Layla. She begged him not to tell the others, knowing they would have pulled the plug on the whole thing if they knew and even if Martinez was willing to go behind his friend's back to get Alexa in without him, there was no way of knowing if they would get another opportunity.

There was no indication that Martinez's words had registered as Dante heeded Layla's call, rushing to stand before the thick pane of glass that separated them.

Layla tilted her head coyly, looking up at Dante through her lashes. With a shaky hand, he reached for the intercom.

"God, Layla, I'm so fucking sorry," he said, unable to take his eyes from her. She was still his Layla, but different. The glow in her eyes was just as bright as Ethan's had been, but somehow she didn't look like a rabid dog like he thought Ethan did. If anything, he thought her more beautiful than he remembered.

"None of this is your fault, Dante. My sweet Dante," she said, pressing closer to the barrier between them. "I'm still me. I've missed you so much. Thinking of you was the only thing that kept me going," she continued, swiping at her eyes as if she were crying. But no moisture appeared. Unfortunately, Dante didn't seem to notice or care.

"Martinez, open the door, man," Dante commanded.

"Come on, Dante, you know I can't," he replied, pulling the tranquilizer out and slipping it behind his back. He moved directly between Dante and the control panel, only taking a moment to glance at Alexa still in Ethan's cell; the couple sitting calmly on the floor staring at one another.

He'd been watching intently as Alexa entered, trying to ascertain the level of threat Ethan represented. He'd been like a broken animal when she entered, cowering in the corner until she actually offered him her blood. Once he bit her, Martinez knew it was over. No matter what Ethan did after that, he couldn't open the door again until it was certain that neither of them was infected. That was when he'd turned his focus to Dante and Layla.

"Open the fucking door!" Dante commanded with a growl, dropping his hand and turning to his friend. Martinez cursed under his breath. That look in Dante's eyes told him he was going to need the syringe and nothing short of a miracle to keep the cell closed. Dante was a far superior warrior and they both knew it. Martinez's only advantage was surprise, or so he thought.

In a blur of motion, Dante was on him. Before Martinez could even react, he was pinned to the wall with the syringe intended for Dante jammed securely in his side.

"Sorry, bro, I have to do this," Dante whispered before letting Martinez's limp body slide to the floor. When the three of them were sneaking into the containment wing, Dante had continued to absorb Alexa's telepathy. While she was far too strong for him to dig into her mind without her knowing, Martinez's shields were weakened while he focused his own ability to conceal the group. So Dante knew his best friend planned to keep him from Layla; part of him was glad for it. Deep down, he knew the risk she posed, but one look at her and he didn't care about that anymore.

He glanced toward Alexa and Ethan and his heart ached at seeing the love that was so obvious between them. Ethan's eyes were clear; he was cured and that was all Dante needed to know. There was still hope. He didn't know how long it might take, but they would find a cure, they had to. And if they didn't, he wasn't going to leave Layla to suffer her fate alone. He couldn't abandon her again.

With a deep breath, he slid the lever to open Layla's cell. Using every ounce of his speed, he closed the distance between them, pushing Layla back into the cell before she could make her escape. Being infected, she was stronger than he was and could have easily gotten around him, but luckily she was also teetering on the brink of bloodlust and couldn't resist the call of his blood.

When her fangs tore into his flesh, Dante didn't flinch; instead relaxing into her embrace as he heard the door, which he knew would automatically reset after a few seconds, close behind them. Even though he immediately felt the infection burning its way through his blood, Dante was relieved. No matter what happened next, his life was permanently linked to Layla's and that thought gave him comfort.

CHAPTER 6 - *An Unexpected Transformation*

"What more do I have to do? Why can't you just change me now? Then I could be of even greater use; I could fight beside you and it would be so much easier for me to bring humans for us to enjoy," Molly implored while Lucias wiped the blood from his mouth and slipped back into his custom-made trousers.

"Be patient, pet," Lucias replied, adjusting his again-growing erection and making his way to the door. It had been a while since they had enjoyed the delights of tormenting a helpless human in the playroom they shared; a sacrifice he made for Chloe's benefit, for the time being. Once they completed the blood bond and she became his mate, he would teach her to enjoy the thrill of killing, or he would force her to endure it anyway.

He glanced back over his shoulder at Molly lying naked on the bed, covered in blood with no hint of modesty in her as she left herself completely exposed to his gaze. The sight made him reconsider leaving.

"Turning you will take a great toll on me and I cannot afford to be weak now," Lucias lied, surprisingly not irritated by Molly's questioning him. She pleased him greatly, perhaps more than any creature, living or dead, ever had and a few lies here and there to appease her seemed a small price to pay for that pleasure. "When I have defeated The Elite once and for all, you will have all you desire."

He was almost sad when he realized that it wouldn't be long before she figured out that vampires were only born, not turned. As much as Lucias ached to see her become like him, it was impossible and, when she figured that out, he assumed he would be forced to kill her. After all, she was a vicious little thing; she would seek revenge for his lies, of that he was certain, and he couldn't risk her doing anything that might jeopardize his plans. Not when he was so close.

Molly watched until Lucias disappeared through the door, then she hurried to shower and dress, knowing that she didn't have much time before he would seek out her company again.

It had taken every ounce of her willpower to conceal her anger from Lucias, but she had played her part perfectly, letting him use her body while her mind remained focused on revenge.

He thinks he can just replace me with that wretched bitch? she thought, slipping a blade, one of those she and Lucias often used on the humans she brought home, into a sheath she'd stolen from the weapons stores before she concealed it carefully in the waist of her pants.

She'd noticed the change in Lucias the moment he'd returned with Chloe. Though she only got a quick glance at her before was spirited off to a secured area of the facility, Molly knew Lucias went to see Chloe each day. And now she knew his true intentions.

After all he had promised her, after all she had done for him, he was going to make that little bitch his queen in her place.

Asana paced in her quarters, praying that she hadn't been wrong to let Molly overhear her conversation with Kaleb. She felt the panic of self-doubt creeping in and considered rushing to Chloe's quarters on more than one occasion, but the visions had been clear and she knew it was the only way to keep Chloe safe from Lucias for good.

She was so wound up and anxious about what was to come that she jumped at the soft tap on the door before she rushed to open it.

"I don't like this," Kaleb said, rushing in. Asana placed a finger to her lips, signaling him to be quiet while she closed the door and engaged the sound-proofing.

"The cameras?" she whispered in question.

"There will be no evidence of me being here now," he replied.

"I know; I don't either, but it's the only way," she said as she resumed her pacing.

"We should have told her," Kaleb continued. "What if Molly actually gets to her, what if…?" Kaleb's voice trailed off as if he couldn't even let himself say it.

"It's a miracle she hasn't seen it already, but if she knew, I'm afraid she would try to change it. She would sacrifice herself to your father just like she did before."

Of course, Kaleb knew she was right. Chloe was nothing if not selfless.

But it wasn't just concern for Chloe that had him so anxious. The thought of what was to become of Molly made his stomach turn, but if Asana's visions were true, it was a reality he would have to accept to get what he truly desired most in the world.

"Tell me again about how it happens. Please," Kaleb requested, his voice low as he leaned back against the wall ready to absorb every precious syllable Asana was about to share.

Asana couldn't help but smile despite her anxiety. Even if she hadn't been a seer, Kaleb's feelings for Chloe would have been impossible to miss. It was a miracle his father didn't suspect anything; a blessing she feared would soon run out.

A loud buzz pulled Chloe from her thoughts. It wasn't like Lucias to announce himself; he usually just entered her room, always trying to demonstrate that he was in control, and as she had learned from reading his mind, ever hopeful he would catch a glimpse of her changing. She could feel the bile rising in her throat as she remembered some of the disgusting thoughts Lucias had been having about her. As useful as it was to dig into his mind, she'd been avoiding it more often than not since he seemed intent on keeping his fantasies at the forefront whenever he was in her presence.

Lucias was growing impatient and, though he was no match for Chloe and her abilities, with each passing day her fear increased. Not for herself, but for those she loved.

After a few moments, when the door remained closed, Chloe approached, focusing her telepathy. Though the room was soundproof, she could still read thoughts, but for some reason she couldn't get a clear lock on her visitor. Her heart pounded as she hoped that somehow, some way it was Kaleb, even though she knew it was too great a risk for him to visit her.

When she turned the handle, Molly immediately pushed inside, her presence both a surprise and disappointment to Chloe. She'd never actually met the human who lived among so many infected vampires, but she'd seen enough in Lucias's thoughts to know Molly was not a kind woman.

"Hello," Chloe said tentatively. Even without any barriers, she couldn't get a clear read on Molly. Her thoughts were erratic, each running into the next, making it impossible for Chloe to lock in on her intentions, but she was obviously agitated as she closed the door with her light eyes darting around the room.

"I'm Molly. Lucias sent me to you," Molly lied, eyeing Chloe intently. She made no attempt to mask her contempt as she raked her eyes up and down Chloe's tall frame. Chloe was easily four inches taller, and the most powerful vampire ever born, yet Molly's presence set a chill in her blood.

"I don't understand. Why would he send you to me?" Chloe asked, taking a step back as Molly inched closer.

"To feed you," she replied taking another step forward.

"I'm sorry, there's been a mistake. I, I don't drink live blood," Chloe apologized, her eyes growing wide when Molly pulled the hidden blade from her pants and sliced into her own arm.

Chloe covered her nose and mouth with shock when the sweet scent of Molly's blood invaded her nostrils and forced her fangs down. She'd never been around live human blood before and the aroma was more enticing than she could have ever imagined.

Chloe fled to the farthest wall, trying to put as much distance as possible between her and Molly, who watched with a triumphant smile.

"I've been told it is amazing, drinking live," Molly continued as she moved towards Chloe.

"Please, just leave," Chloe begged without looking back, her voice strained from the pain of her sudden hunger for Molly's blood.

It was just the opportunity Molly was looking for. Without another word, she rushed forward, her eyes wild with fury as she swung the blade, wildly aiming for the back of Chloe's neck.

In that flash of a moment before the steel made contact, Molly's rage and thoughts were completely focused on her plan to kill Chloe, giving the young telepath just enough warning to defend herself from the attack. She spun around, moving so fast that Molly's human eyes couldn't process the motion until, instead of sinking the blade into Chloe's neck, she found herself flying back, the force of Chloe's kick lifting her several inches off the ground before she slammed into door.

With rage still pulsing through her body, Molly tried to stand, intent on carrying out her plans; but as she breathed in with the effort, no air came. She gasped, and then coughed, sending a spray of blood into the air. She grasped for her chest, confused and disoriented when her hand pushed against the blade which was planted firmly in the side of her chest just below her breast.

Chloe stared with wide eyes as Molly attempted to yell out with the pain, but she couldn't take in enough air to manage it. The force with which the human had fallen, coupled with the angle of the blade in her hand, succeeded in puncturing her lung. More blood poured from Molly's mouth as she tried again to move, and her eyes started to roll back.

Chloe ran to her, holding her breath to avoid taking in the scent of Molly's blood, which grew stronger with each passing moment as the vital liquid continued to spill from her wound.

Despite what Molly had just attempted, and all that Chloe knew about what kind of person she was, she couldn't just sit there and watch her die. Chloe could feel Molly's agony as her own, the silent screams of her pain ringing inside both their minds and, despite herself, she gasped, taking in the scent of blood, again causing her fangs to drop even further.

She placed her hands on Molly's chest near the blade, focusing her healing ability. The pain she felt through Molly's mind was enough to help her resist the blood that was covering her hands as she tried to save the life of the woman who wanted her dead.

"Listen to me, Molly!" Chloe yelled, leaning closer to the woman who was inching closer to death with each shallow breath, despite the flow of healing power that was pulsing through her hands. She was bleeding out faster than Chloe could heal her and Chloe knew she didn't have much time left.

Shortly after Chloe healed Alexa, who had been long dead by the time her body was returned to the compound, the pair ventured out to the stables, hoping to share a ride as they continued to get reacquainted, only to discover Chloe's favorite horse lying dead in the stall. She tried for hours to revive the animal to no avail until Alexa finally tore her away, exhausted and defeated. Curious about the extent and limitations of her powers, Commander Claesson and his team of scientists had called on her when some of their injured men were returned to the compound learning she could only resurrect other vampires, and even then only if their central nervous system remained intact, meaning there was no coming back from a head shot or decapitation. Humans and animals, it seemed, could only be healed before the point of death; once they were gone, there was no coming back.

"You have to drink my blood," Chloe yelled, not sure if Molly could even hear her, biting into her own wrist and pressing it to Molly's bluish lips. In her training back on The Elite compound, she'd learned that vampire blood could speed human healing. She just prayed it was enough to buy her the time she needed to seal Molly's wounds.

Molly had already lost consciousness, but desperate, Chloe kept her wrist against the ghost-white woman's lips, her vampire blood dripping down porcelain skin and mingling with the crimson already staining Molly's blouse. She kept her wrist there, doing everything she could to get the blood into Molly's system while she continued focusing her power to stitch the broken flesh back together. She kept trying, even after her preternatural hearing could no longer detect the faint flutter of Molly's heartbeat.

All Chloe wanted was for Molly to wake up. She was a pure, gentle soul and the weight of causing the death of another living creature pressed on her like nothing she had ever experienced before. Yes, she had used her powers to disable infected soldiers before, and they were ultimately killed as a result, but she hadn't killed them; they hadn't died by her hand. Somehow this was different. Molly was human; she was weak, almost defenseless against a vampire, let alone one as powerful as Chloe. And while everything that Kaleb and Asana had told her, and all the glimpses of Molly she'd caught in Lucias's mind indicated that she was evil, twisted, Chloe believed there was good in her. She believed there was good in everyone, almost. After all her time in Lucias's mind, she had yet to find evidence of good in him.

Time seemed to be standing still as she stayed there, her wrist still pressed to Molly's lips even though the punctures she'd made had long healed closed.

Her guilt was so powerful that she didn't even feel the usual surge of fear when she sensed that Lucias was near. He entered, unannounced, but remained eerily silent just inside the door as he took in the carnage of Chloe's quarters. His mind was swimming with unfamiliar emotions. The scent of death hung heavy in the air; there was no denying that Molly was dead.

"What have you done?" he whispered, stepping closer and getting a full view of Molly's bloody, lifeless body cradled gently in Chloe's arms. Chloe wasn't certain if the question was directed at her or Molly. Even as rage and something altogether unfamiliar, actual sadness, washed over him, Lucias's fangs dropped from his gums and his cock began to fill. It was the blood. Both the scent of it in the air and the sight of it covering Chloe's beautiful form as she clutched the remains of her first kill turned him on.

He'd lost a precious possession in the process, but he had already resolved himself to that inevitability. The fact that Molly was even there in Chloe's room was evidence of that. Still, he felt the loss as much as someone like him could, but he pushed those emotions back and simply waited in silence.

After several minutes, Chloe gently moved Molly's body away. Bile rose up in her throat as she glanced at Lucias; his growing desire apparent in the tenting of his expensive pants and the blaring thoughts in his head. She cringed at seeing her own image in his mind resembling some tormented ghost from a horror movie between the tears covering her face, her skin left pale by the events of the last hour and a mixture of Molly's blood and her own covering the front of her cream-colored dress. Using speed, which made her nearly impossible for Lucias to track, she moved into the bathroom and closed and locked the door behind her.

Chloe screamed out her frustration, the mirror in front of her shattering as it was assaulted by her rising power. She stripped away her stained clothes, stepping into the shower and turning it on full blast, not caring that it was freezing cold or that it was very soon going to be scalding hot. She hated that Lucias was hovering outside and would never have shown him such weakness or showered with him anywhere nearby, but her need to remove the proof of what she had done far outweighed her fear of him.

Lucias paced just outside the door, focusing his senses on Chloe inside and, despite the alien feelings of grief for Molly tugging at him, he smiled.

Chloe had killed, the act stripping away a layer of innocence which had separated her from him. Now she was vulnerable, uncertain of herself, but somehow stronger, more powerful. He didn't possess the power of telepathy, or any special ability for that matter, but even he could sense the change. This was his chance, perhaps the only one he would get.

His cock grew harder as he listened to the slow strum of Chloe's heartbeat amidst the droplets of water he envisioned pouring over her perfect naked form only a few feet away. Only one locked door stood between him and the object of his desire, the barrier providing no real challenge for a determined vampire. He could be inside the room, and Chloe, practically before she knew what had happened.

Perhaps she will not even fight it. He thought, reaching for the handle, his heart speeding with anticipation and desire.

"What happened?" Lucias's head snapped around to the source of the gravelly voice, his eyes wide with shock at first and then, when he realized what he was seeing, pure joy. "I'm so thirsty," Molly continued grabbing her throat, her blue eyes glowing with the unmistakable power of his kind.

CHAPTER 7 - *Discovery*

"How could you let him do this?" Rachel asked, her voice still rough after spending the past hour unconscious on Cami's bathroom floor thanks to the tranquilizer with which her good friend had injected her.

"If it makes you feel any better, you're not the only one who got knocked out," Jared said, referring to the guard in Jasmine's bathroom, trying to be funny, but falling short of the target and earning irritated glares from both women.

"Jared, can you give us a few minutes alone?" Cami asked, looking at him pointedly. As much as he hated leaving her for even a second, he slipped out the door.

"That's the point, Rach, we didn't let him. We kidnapped and threatened you to make him help us, at least that's what Dante and

Alexa are going to tell Commander Claesson," Cami said, offering her a bag of blood before she slipped to the door and engaged the soundproofing, not wanting Jared listening in as he was undoubtedly doing. "We told Martinez we would cover for him, we just didn't mention how. It wouldn't work if someone saw you wandering free around the compound. He'll understand when you tell him."

"The only thing he's going to understand, when he hears that you drugged me and hid me away, is anger. Oh, God; he'll probably challenge Dante! He'll never win and then he'll be shipped off in Dante's place or worse." Rachel responded, panic lacing her voice.

"I mean, when you tell him about the baby, Rach."

"But, how did you...?"

Cami smiled warmly at her friend and placed her hand on her shoulder. "You've been glowing for days," Cami offered in explanation, "and according to Jared, you're a loud broadcaster. It seems you've been thinking of nothing else since you found out."

She pulled Rachel into a warm embrace, evidence of how much she had changed since meeting Jared. In all the years the two women had known each other, Cami had never hugged Rachel before.

"So you understand why we couldn't let him take the fall for anything we've done. Dante loves Layla and Ethan is my brother, so it's worth it for us, but you're going to need Martinez; your baby is going to need him."

"What about Jared? How in the hell did you get him to agree to this craziness? Even if it works and Ethan is cured, you and Dante are going to be punished. Claesson will figure out that you helped, you know how he is. Don't you remember for how long he sent you away last time?" Rachel asked, the concern for her friend evident.

"Jared doesn't know. At least he doesn't fully understand, but it was a risk I had to take for my brother. I'm praying Chloe was right and, if Ethan is cured, Commander Claesson will be too busy to dig into it and if not, maybe he'll be lenient and only sentence us to a couple of years down South."

"Jared is going to be furious, Cami. You should have told him the truth. Going down there will be easier on you than on him; you'll be kept busy while he'll be stuck back here with nothing but his worry to keep him company."

Cami was well aware of how angry Jared was going to be when he learned that the standard punishment for an infraction of this magnitude was a sentence in The Elite's most notorious compound, located in Antarctica. Given the nature of the terrain and the weather down there, it was The Elite's most secure and most dreaded facility with only one way in and out. Cami knew it well; she'd spent five years there in the early 1900s. Back then it hadn't been so bad, hardly any different from life on the compound in Indy as far as she was concerned, apart from the dreadful cold, but that was before; before she was in love. She really wasn't sure how she could abide being separated from Jared for any length of time, but Ethan was her brother and he needed her help. She had lost him for so long before; she couldn't bear it again.

"There is another option," Cami whispered, receiving a shocked look from Rachel in return.

Everyone in The Elite was surprised by Cami's relationship with Jared, even Rachel, given her generally cold nature over the decades; but despite the rapid thaw in her demeanor over the past few weeks, it was unfathomable to think she would consider the only alternative to a sentence at the South Pole.

"You would consider that?"

"For him? Yes. It isn't even really a choice anymore; he is my life now," Cami replied, certain in her decision. She only hoped the Commander would let it stand if it came to that. "And what about you; what will you do when the baby comes?"

Rachel and Martinez were crossing into uncharted waters, being the first mated pair in The Elite and now the first parents. There were no clear rules on the subject, but it was hard to imagine a child growing up in such an environment. The Commander's own daughter was a rare presence on the compound; having a civilian mother allowed them to live in a nearby colony where he visited as often as possible, but it would be harder for Rachel and Martinez. One of them would have to turn their back on virtually the only life they had known, and deciding which would not be an easy task, given the value of each of their unique abilities.

"I honestly don't know. Obviously, I have to tell John first. I can hardly bear the thought of living separately if only one of us stays on here; but how can we raise a child on the compound?"

The soldiers had tempered their behavior and language as much as possible while Chloe was around, but her childhood lasted only days, not the years it would take a typical vampire child to mature. The alternative would be for both of them to leave The Elite and join a colony or make a home amongst the humans, but that would not be without challenges. They had lived the strict lives of soldiers for decades, centuries even. Living and working amongst civilians, vampire or human, would require an incredible amount of adjustment, especially when it came to making a living. While the life of an Elite soldier was strict, they enjoyed many of the finer things in life as reward. A comparable career in the civilian sector required a skill set and education neither of them possessed.

"All of the planning and consideration in the world could very well be in vain. There is a good chance that none of us will be alive to worry about it," Rachel stated, her tone flat as she placed her hand over the tiny life deep within her belly, and her eyes welled up with tears. She'd never considered having children before she fell in love with John Martinez, having resolved herself to a soldier's life; but now that it had happened, she wanted nothing more than to see her child come into the world.

Cami took Rachel's hand, another unexpected display of affection and intimacy. "Rachel, I wish I had answers for you, but nothing is certain now. All I can tell you is that I will do everything in my power to protect you and make sure that this world is one you want to bring your child into."

"Thanks, Cami," Rachel replied with a weak smile.

"I hate to do this now, but we need your help with one more tiny detail," Cami said, holding her thumb and forefinger together to indicate how small a favor it was, though the look on her face implied that it was a pretty big one.

"What?" Rachel asked suspiciously.

"There's a soldier in Jasmine's bathroom who's going to need some new memories before we can let him go," she replied with a shrug.

"Fine, but if we survive all this, you're going to owe me at least a week of free babysitting," she teased, happy to do whatever was necessary to help her friends.

"I still cannot help but think this is a dream," Ethan whispered as he stroked Alexa's cheek. He had not taken his hands off of her since their first contact, too afraid that she would disappear to let her go even for a moment.

"I assure you this is no dream, my love," Alexa replied with eyes full of love and devotion. Under Ethan's gentle touch, she felt like herself again for the first time since Chloe healed her and her true vampire nature was released. It was strange, but being separated from Ethan seemed to have had a far greater impact than dying and being resurrected as a vampire had.

"I'm so sorry, Amor," Ethan whispered as he began to sob, sinking into Alexa's embrace and seeking comfort he knew he didn't deserve.

How could she ever forgive him?

Alexa placed her hands on the sides of his face and urged him up to look at her, wiping away the tears with her thumbs as he moved. "My sweet Ethan, none of this was your fault. You can't control fate any more than I can command the stars. I am awed by you and your strength; to have lived with all of this for so long, bearing it all alone. You are amazing and I love you more than words can say."

He opened his mouth to respond, but unable to resist any longer, Alexa slammed her mouth onto his in a kiss that told him what her words could not. The kiss was like coming home and finding something new and exciting all at once. Alexa was different as a vampire and losing each other had made their love as strong as any that had ever come before it. They gave everything to each other in that kiss; passion, love, understanding, forgiveness. It was like a signature on the contract of their renewed bond.

Ethan deepened the kiss, a new hunger forming at having Alexa back in his arms; her body familiar, but changed. She was a bit thinner than he remembered, but not without the luscious curves he adored. And she was stronger; he could sense the immense new power in her and it thrilled him in a way he'd never expected.

Alexa pulled back, panting as she gazed into Ethan's eyes that were darkened by his growing desire. Her stomach clenched with need at seeing the look in his eyes, but it wasn't the time or the place for that.

As much as she wished she could stay there forever in that moment with Ethan, Alexa stood pulling him with her, not that she needed to pull him. His hooded green-gray eyes tracked every flinch, every flex of muscle and his body followed as if tethered to her by hundreds of invisible strings. He could not lose her again. He would not lose her again, not even for a moment.

The emotion and excitement of finally being with Ethan and seeing him cured exactly as Chloe's vision had predicted had distracted Alexa temporarily from the dull ache in her heart. That of a mother worried for her child.

Despite her obvious arousal and hesitation, with their bond fully restored and Lucias's wretched infection washed from his system, Ethan didn't need for Alexa to voice the concern that glistened in her eyes.

"We will get her back," he stated, his tone indicating that his words were indeed fact. While he worried for their daughter, Ethan felt a sense of freedom that he had not known since he was a child. Ironic, since he was still locked in a cell, but the prophecy, which had hung over his head his entire life, had indeed been fulfilled, at least his part in it had. Every detail that had terrified him into a life of solitude had come to pass. He'd found his soul mate, borne a child of immense power, and lost the woman he loved by his own hand, all as had been foretold, all as he had feared, and by some miracle he had come out on the other side with Alexa back in his arms. He was absolved; finally free to live his life without the dark cloud that knowing one's own future inevitably presented.

And there was something else. He'd made a promise to Lucias. A promise he would now be able to keep.

Alexa lifted her chin and squared her shoulders, drawing strength from Ethan and their bond. He was right. Chloe was strong, perhaps stronger than anyone, human or vampire, who had ever lived. Chloe would hold Lucias at bay until they could save her. There was no other future she could let herself envision.

She took Ethan's hand and they turned, ready to face whatever life threw at them next, together.

Between the soundproof barrier of the cell and Ethan and Alexa's focus on each other, they hadn't noticed what went down with Dante and Martinez.

Seeing Martinez lying unconscious on the floor, Alexa rushed to the glass with Ethan in tow.

"Oh no," she whispered, knowing that her suspicions about Dante had been confirmed.

"What is it?" Ethan asked, squeezing her hand gently, trying to offer comfort as he shared her anxiety through their bond. Before, he would have put up shields to block some of the sensations, but after everything that had happened, after losing Alexa once, Ethan wanted to feel and savor every moment of their connection to the fullest.

"One of the soldiers who helped me get to you is in love with the woman who came here with you, the one in the next cell. We all hoped he would be able to resist, but he must have gone in there with her. She was infected, but they were not bonded. If he's in there, he'll be infected and it could put the entire compound at risk if either of them gets out."

Ethan glanced toward the barrier that separated his cell from Layla's; his eyes filling with guilt and regret as images of their time together flashed in his mind. Alexa looked at him, feeling the shift in his demeanor.

"Can you hear their minds?" he asked quickly, trying to divert her attention before she probed further. He would tell her everything, just not yet. He'd just gotten her back.

Alexa nodded and focused on the other enclosure, searching for Dante's stream of consciousness. She found it easily, but was surprised by the state of his mind and her own response to it.

She wobbled back, falling into Ethan, who looked down at her first with concern, then with eyes darkened by desire as the scent of Alexa's arousal filled the small space.

"He's in there with her, they're locked in together and he's infected," she said breathlessly.

"Alexa?" Ethan queried, his tone full of questions while his eyes zeroed in on her full lips, desperate to kiss her as her arousal became his own through their connection.

The reason didn't matter; he couldn't fight the pull and lowered his lips to hers. This kiss was hungry, demanding; a reflection of the desire burning through their bond and growing more desperate with each stroke of his tongue against hers. Alexa panted beneath him and let out a moan that kicked his arousal even higher. In a blur, they were against the wall and Ethan had her hands pinned above her head as he conquered her mouth, pouring all of the lust and need for her that had built up over the weeks into his kiss. If she couldn't feel it in that, or even through their bond, the steel-hard length he pressed against her stomach as he moved against her was evidence enough of how deeply he wanted her.

"Ethan, I…," Alexa whispered breathlessly against his lips.

"Sorry to interrupt, but I think the jig is up," Martinez said through the intercom, startling them both.

The security lights were flashing throughout the room as Martinez opened the door.

Blushing, Alexa stepped out and hugged Martinez with one arm while she continued to hold Ethan's hand with the other. Ethan growled behind her, his eyes glowing as he glared at the man who dared to touch Alexa.

"Ethan, this is John Martinez; he's a good friend of mine and Cami's. He's responsible for getting me in here to you," she said, squeezing his hand.

"Sorry, man; I'm seriously just a friend," Martinez said as he stepped back and raised his arms in mock surrender. "You were right about Dante," he said to Alexa. "I tried to stop him, but, well, see for yourself," he continued, gesturing to the neighboring cell but keeping his eyes on Ethan, who looked ready to pounce on him at slightest provocation.

Alexa and Ethan stepped over to get a view. She immediately swiveled and covered her eyes as the blush that was already covering her cheeks deepened several shades.

"Yeah, it's a bit much to take in," Martinez said with a smirk, trying to mask his sadness as he leaned against the wall for support, still not fully recovered from the tranquilizer. "I guess if he's going to go, there are worse ways to do it."

Ethan pulled Alexa into his arms, and as much as he hated it, pushed up his mental shields to lessen the impact of their bond. It was all he could think to do as he watched Layla and Dante writhing naked on the floor, covered in each other's blood.

He hated lying to her, but what choice did he have? He'd just gotten her back and he couldn't risk having her find out this way. He would tell her what happened with Layla, but it would have to wait for a better time.

Alexa faced him, immediately sensing the change. Her lips parted; the question on the tip of her tongue as the alarm sounded, forcing them all to cover their ears.

Jared paced the hallway outside Cami's quarters. He'd understood her need to speak with Rachel alone, considering the delicate nature of the subject and his short acquaintance with Martinez's mate, but it drove him crazy nonetheless. Especially when he heard the soundproofing to her room engage. It didn't help that he had a nagging feeling that Cami was hiding something from him and he was seriously regretting his promise to not read her thoughts without her permission; based on recent history that limited him to using the ability during sex. He'd attempted to sneak a peek into her mind a few times, but she'd become attuned to the sensation and learned to reinforce her mental shields, keeping him out.

Several minutes had passed and he was starting to get anxious. It had been a while since they'd left the others at the containment unit and he was growing increasingly worried for his sister and friends. He focused and searched for Cami with his mind, but was met with silence.

He reached for the intercom, but yanked his hand back and covered his ears when an alarm sounded throughout the compound. In his attempt to hear Chloe, he'd unwittingly amped up his preternatural hearing so the blare of the alarm was deafening.

Before he could react further, Cami flung her door open and rushed out with Rachel attempting to follow, but Cami froze in the doorway before Rachel was in sight of the corridor security camera.

"Sorry, Rach, but if our story about Martinez is going to be convincing, you can't come rushing in with the rest of us. Just hang back for five minutes, and act groggy when you get there," Cami said, facing away from the camera to hide the fact that she was speaking.

"I don't think I'll have to act; I'm still feeling a little off. What the hell did you give me?" Rachel responded, not bothering to hide the irritation in her voice.

Cami didn't say anything, knowing that she would have been livid if the situation had been reversed. Instead, she turned, gave Rachel a reassuring smile, and pulled the door closed before she gave her attention to Jared.

The pair didn't speak, only exchanging a knowing glance before they flashed away to the containment unit. Standard Elite protocol was for Cami to report to the pit and await the Commander's orders, but there was really no point. She knew the source of the alarm and, if the security footage was reviewed, it would probably reveal her part in the current state of chaos, leaving her with a life-altering choice to make so, fuck protocol. She needed to know what happened to Ethan, Alexa, and the others, and Jared wanted no less.

It only took a couple of minutes for the pair to travel the distance to the containment unit and the ensuing pandemonium that was just outside the door. Clearly, Cami hadn't been the only one to ignore protocol.

"How the fuck did this happen!" Commander Claesson roared rhetorically as the guard who'd been assigned to the containment unit cringed in the corner, trying to make himself invisible behind some of the other soldiers.

He'd been just as surprised as anyone when the alarm sounded a few moments after the Commander let one of the scientists into the area. Clearly, something had happened inside, causing the researcher to sound the alarm, but it shut him and the prisoners in until the system reset in five minutes, practically an eternity to a vampire who is in a hurry. Because of the panels that came down, they couldn't even see into the interior corridor.

Cami glanced toward Jared just as the nervous guard caught sight of them. He opened his mouth, but then closed it again when Cami glared at him. His silence wouldn't mean much either way with Jester rounding the corner shortly after, no doubt to report what he'd found on the security footage at the Commander's request. Cami imagined she'd be shipped off before the door even opened, separated from Jared and wondering about her brother and the others for God knew how long.

The Commander locked eyes with Jester, who shrugged his shoulders. "I don't know, sir. The footage for this sector was quiet, exactly as I would expect normally. It showed the guard alone at his post up until you opened the door, then alone again until the moment I came here to report. Inside looks completely normal; just the two prisoners in their cells. If there had been anything out of the ordinary, sir, I would have reported it as it happened."

Cami looked toward the guard again, then at Jared, finding him looking as confused as she did. It made sense, since Jester didn't see anything abnormal in the lab because Dante had implemented the loop on the cameras, a loop Jester had unknowingly provided, but they hadn't tampered with the camera on the outer door. She gave Jared a more pointed look. When his expression remained the same, she nonchalantly tapped her temple while lowering her mental shields.

Understanding dawned on his face and he pushed into her mind.

Can you read Jester's thoughts? Why didn't he mention we were here close to the time all this went down? she asked in her mind.

Jared nodded and turned his attention to The Elite's IT specialist.

Jester glanced at Jared, and then gave Cami a wink.

Shit. Neither of them knew why, but Jester was covering for them. Perhaps he hadn't been as in the dark about why Dante wanted the looping program as they'd thought.

"Smith, you want to tell me exactly what the hell is going on?" Commander Claesson bellowed, his eyes narrowed on the guard who was still a bit groggy.

"I, sir, I just, I…," the confused guard stammered.

"For the love of God; spit it out, man!"

"Sorry, sir," Smith continued, trying to regain his composure. Cami actually felt sorry for him; he had no idea about Martinez's ability, so there was no way he could guard against it. "I'm not really sure what happened; you were here with one of the doctors, he went in, and you left. A few minutes later the alarm started."

As much as he wanted to be pissed, Commander Claesson knew that Smith hadn't done anything wrong. There weren't any signs that the prisoners had escaped, so they were just going to have to wait for the system to reset. Meanwhile, a number of fucked up scenarios were running through the Commander's head, all of which involved his own men, and made his eye twitch.

Cami let out a sigh of relief at hearing Smith's explanation. For whatever reason, he'd decided to leave out the fact that she and Jared just happened to have replaced the assigned blood courier within an hour of the disturbance; not that it was proof of their involvement on its own, but it wouldn't take much digging for a man like Claesson to put all the pieces together. Now she would at least be able to find out what had happened on the other side of the door they were all watching with fear and anticipation, before she had to deal with the consequences of her involvement.

She had to assume that Dante and Martinez were still inside; no amount of altered security footage or omitted details could hide their part now. The plan was for them to sneak back out under the cover of Martinez's mist when the next scientist entered; regardless of what happened with Ethan and Alexa, they were going to lock her in. If that had been the case, the scientist inside wouldn't have pulled the alarm. He would have alerted the Commander and other researchers more discreetly. The alarm indicated that he felt that there was an immediate threat that needed to be contained.

After what felt like an eternity, the alarm stopped and the system reset. Everyone in the hallway, soldiers and civilians alike, looked around at one another with expressions of anxiety and expectation.

Without a word, Commander Claesson flashed to the door where several of the resident scientists were already gathered, and checked the weapon in his hands, which was loaded with heavy tranquilizers, and then his side arm, which was loaded with actual bullets. He prayed that he wouldn't need the back-up gun. Claesson quickly entered the security code and lowered his head for the retinal scan to gain entry to the containment unit. "Dr. Jones, come with me, everyone else wait here," he ordered as the door slid open and immediately closed behind them before anyone could object.

Cami pushed her way to the entrance, with Jared close on her heels. "Fuck!" she yelled, startling most of the people in the general vicinity.

Jared reached up and stroked her temple gently, indicating that he wanted to hear what she was thinking.

Cami sighed and looked up into his eyes. As hard as it was for her, she was learning to be vulnerable with him, to let him see and hear what was in her head and heart.

I'm so afraid of what we're going to find in there. I'm not sure I can bare it if Alexa was wrong, if Ethan isn't cured. They could all be infected now, or worse.

Jared pulled her into his arms, surprised by how willingly she came, given all the people surrounding them, and kissed the top of her head. He understood her fears; he shared them.

If Ethan or Layla were out of their cells, it was more than likely that Commander Claesson would have no choice but to use deadly force against them, given the great advantages of strength and speed the infection gave them. Not to mention the fact that Ethan was already stronger and faster than any vampire the ancient Commander had ever encountered. With the short amount of time that had passed and the lack of human blood to fuel the transformation, if the others were infected, they would be easily incapacitated by the tranquilizers and, though their use could have damaging effects on their transitioning bodies, it was better than the alternative

"Ethan, we have to get back in your cell; they're coming," Alexa stated, pushing him back towards the door as the thick silver-plated panels rose; her voice laced with panic as she sensed the Commander drawing near. Due to the current state of mind he was in, he was likely to shoot all of them before they had a chance to explain, so the cell was the safest place. There had been so much happening when the scientist spotted them and pulled the alarm outside, that she hadn't sensed his approach in time. She shot a glance over her shoulder at Martinez, who opened the door. As he was about to pull the lever to close them in, Alexa continued. "I'm so sorry, John, but we did what we could to protect you. Tell the Commander we forced you. Dante and I took Rachel and threatened to hurt her if you didn't help us."

"No one's going to believe that," he replied, looking nervous as his eyes went to the door where the Commander would soon appear.

"They'll believe it because part of it is true; we *did* take her. We had to so they would believe you. Please just trust me; I will explain everything, but right now you have to close that door and get back against the wall," she pleaded, her heart pounding as she willed the glass, which was the only thing that would keep Ethan safe, to close.

Even as his anger began to rise, Martinez knew better than to refuse. He knew his friends wouldn't hurt Rachel, but the thought of her being involved in any way made his stomach turn. She was everything to him, which is why he didn't have a choice, and he did the only thing he could. He closed the cell, faced the wall, and placed his hands behind his head.

A second later, the outer door opened and Commander Claesson barreled in with weapons drawn and anger pouring off of him in palpable waves.

He looked around the room, stopping on Martinez's back along with the aim of his weapon. "Have you been exposed?" he growled.

"No, sir." Martinez replied immediately.

"Turn around slowly and show me your eyes."

Martinez did as commanded. Claesson pulled a set of silver-plated handcuffs from his belt and tossed them towards Dr. Jones, whose gaze was so focused on Ethan's cell that they hit his arm and fell to the floor. He jumped in surprise before the scientist who'd pulled the alarm scooped them up. "Put those on him and loop them through that pipe over there, just in case," Claesson ordered, pointing to the metal rod in the corner. When it was done, he holstered his weapon and turned his attention to the cells.

He scanned Ethan's, then Layla's. "Motherfucker," he said to no one in particular, as he took in the scene unfolding in the cell on the right, knowing that the four in the cells couldn't hear him. It was impossible to tell, given the amount of blood and the tangle of naked limbs thrashing around. "Is it safe to assume that that's Dante in there with her?" he asked of Martinez, as he gestured to the couple.

"Yes, sir. I tried to stop him, sir, but—"

"Shut the fuck up, Martinez!" Claesson spat. Disgusted, he stormed over to the glass where Alexa was waiting and pressed the button to talk to her, though with how he was feeling, he was pretty sure he could produce a yell loud enough for it to be heard through the barrier.

"What the fuck were you thinking?" he bellowed, his eyes going to her bloodied wrist. "He bit you?? Why the fuck didn't you listen, Alexa? Now another one of my men has this filthy virus and you'll be infected any moment, too!"

"I'm sorry, for all of this," she replied softly, as she looked to the wall separating her from Dante and Layla. "But he's my husband, my mate; I had to save him."

Claesson opened his mouth, but then snapped it shut as Ethan placed a gentle hand on Alexa's shoulder and gave him a hard look. "She's not infected, sir. And thanks to her, and her friends, neither am I."

The Commander looked back toward the doctor, who was still shocked by the discovery that he'd been noticed and had been watching since they'd entered the room.

Hearing Ethan refer to Alexa's friends served only to remind the Commander that not one, but two of his men, had disobeyed his direct order, regardless of the outcome of their disobedience, and reignited his anger. Sensing that, Alexa spoke up again. "It was all my idea, Commander. I used Dante's feelings for Layla to persuade him to help me, and we forced Martinez. He didn't have a choice; we took Rachel and threatened to hurt her if he didn't help. I had to do it; no one would believe me if I didn't show you," she blurted.

"This is utterly remarkable," Dr. Jones said, moving closer to the cell as he stared at Ethan's eyes, which no longer showed any sign of infection. "I'll, of course, need to take a blood sample, but he seems to be completely cured. And he actually bit you?" he asked of Alexa, who nodded her affirmation "Sir, she would certainly be showing signs of infection by now if she had the virus. To be sure, I'll need to confer with the rest of the team and we'll need to collect samples and interview these two and the others if we can convince them to speak to us; though based on their state, I'd guess it may be a couple of days before the bloodlust subsides. It would be wise to get them some human blood before they hurt each other; a lot of blood," he said, watching the couple with the curious gaze of a scientist.

The good doctor couldn't mask his enthusiasm as he began rushing around the room, gathering materials to collect blood samples, stopping occasionally to tap out notes and mumbling excitedly to himself.

Claesson hated to admit it, but Alexa and Dante's little stunt had just provided the first real breakthrough they'd had in several centuries of researching Lucias's virus.

CHAPTER 8 - *Sex, Love, and Lies*

Lucias remained frozen, staring with eyes full of wonder as Molly struggled to stand. She locked her blue eyes on him, full of confusion and hunger. A wide smile spread across his face. If the change in her eyes hadn't been evidence enough, the shift in her scent was undeniable. She was vampire.

He didn't know how or why, but he'd never been a man to question good fortune. Without a word, Lucias scooped Molly up into his arms and whisked her out of the room and to his playroom, which contained the closest supply of bagged red cells.

"Don't try to speak; just feed" he said to Molly as he stroked her hair and passed her a bag of AB negative from his private stores. She obeyed without hesitation, his eyes darkening with desire as her new fangs punched through her gums, and she closed her eyes, and tore into the thick plastic.

She downed several bags in a matter of minutes before finally stopping and opening her bright eyes to look up at Lucias, who watched her carefully.

"Thank you," she whispered. "I'm so sorry; I, I thought it was all a lie!" she blurted; an edge of panic in her voice for what she had done. Lucias was not a patient or forgiving man; no one knew that as well as Molly, who had witnessed his wrath being visited on countless others during her time with him.

"Shh," he whispered, pushing his hands into her blonde hair, "all is forgiven, my pet." He fisted her hair and yanked her head back hard as his fangs, which had been out since he'd discovered her lifeless body in Chloe's room, dropped even lower. He lowered his head and scraped one sharp point up the length of her neck. "How do you feel now?" he asked, placing both fangs against her artery without breaking the skin, applying just enough pressure for her to feel it and build the anticipation. He'd fed on her more times than he could count, but this was different. He could feel a new power coursing through her veins; Chloe's power; a magnificent and unexpected gift.

"Strong, alive," she husked, straining upwards against Lucias's bite. She wanted it with a desire unlike any she'd ever known; but more than his bite, she wanted to taste his blood, to feel her fangs pierce his flesh and drink in the warmth moving through his body with every slow beat of his vampire heart.

Sensing her need, Lucias bit down, his eyes widening as her life's essence flowed over his tongue. The power was undeniable and his first thought was of how it would taste if taken directly from the source. If Chloe's blood could do this, if she could change an ordinary human into one of their kind, what effect would it have on him? Even as he continued to drink from Molly's neck, his lips turned up in a devious smile at the thought.

He would have everything he had ever dreamed of and more. His wait for Chloe was over. He would take her and make her his, finally completing the bond and reaping all of the benefits of her awesome power.

Releasing Molly's neck, he stood, his mind now focused on Chloe, but before he could take a step, Molly was on him and, using the full force of her new strength, pinned him to the wall next to their rack of toys. She held his arms at his sides with his hands up by his ears and looked at him with a challenging smirk and a question in her eyes as she pressed her hips against his erection.

I've waited this long, it can wait just a while longer. he thought, giving Molly a slight nod before he turned his head and willingly exposed his neck to her. She bit down with a ferocious hunger and desire that only served to increase his own. He'd often wished to see Molly like this, as one of his kind, even though it had only been an impossible fantasy. She took several long pulls on his vein and his eyes drifted to the array of tools lining the wall, his cock hardening further as ideas for their use flashed through his mind. Chloe could definitely wait.

After enduring several minutes under the scalding hot spray of her shower, Chloe accepted that no amount of water could wash away the pain and guilt of what she'd done. With a trembling hand, she turned off the water and stepped out into the steamy fog of the room. Wrapping a towel around her body, she lowered her mental shields slightly and said a prayer of thanks when she found that Lucias had gone. But as quickly as the relief had come, it was chased away by fear and regret. Molly's lifeless body would still be there in her room. It was too much to hope that Lucias would have taken her away. No, indeed, he would like nothing more than for Chloe to be trapped there with the painful reminder of her own darkness until she could no longer stand it and was begging for him to save her from it.

Chloe swiped her hand across the clouded mirror and stared into her own eyes. *No. I can't give in to him.*

Her thoughts turned to Alexa and Ethan and she wondered if they were together as she had foreseen. She smiled even as her eyes welled up with tears, thinking of the joy she knew they would find in being together again. She saw flashes of Jared and Cami, and her grandparents, and all of the soldiers who had tried to protect her, and Asana and her daughter, and finally, she saw Kaleb as clearly as if he was standing right before her. For all of them, for everyone she loved, she couldn't let Lucias win no matter what it cost her in the end. She just wished she knew what that cost would be. Try as she may, she still couldn't see anything past her vision of Lucias bringing Anna there to punish Asana.

Standing up a little straighter with a renewed strength, she stepped out of the bathroom ready to face her demons, both imagined and tangible. Though the floor was stained with blood, hers and Molly's alike, much to Chloe's surprise there was no other sign of her or Lucias. She dressed quickly in a light-colored gown, like always. Despite his dark thoughts and intentions towards her, Lucias liked to dress Chloe like the proverbial virgin in some variation of a white gown that covered her body conservatively. Chloe knew from his thoughts that he liked seeing her as pure so that when he finally corrupted her as he desired, the victory would be that much sweeter.

Fully dressed, she took a deep breath and focused her mind, searching for Kaleb's stream of consciousness. With the surveillance focused on her room, she would need to use every fiber of her supernatural power to move the distance to Kaleb's quarters undetected and she needed for him to have the door open for her in order to avoid the camera in the corridor. They had often talked about sneaking to meet in such a fashion, but one of them was usually sensible enough to talk the other out of it.

Before she could zero in on Kaleb, Chloe stepped back from the door, surprised to hear the steady strum of two heartbeats approaching. Fearful it was Lucias returning, she sped to the other side of the room and concentrated on raising her other powers to the surface. During her time as Lucias's captive, she had been practicing the controlling and calling of her abilities at will. She could now aim her mind blasts, which had once been controlled by her emotions and would impact anyone within range, zeroing in on a single target or group of them.

Her fear quickly melted into relief and then excitement when Asana stepped through the door, followed by Kaleb. Without hesitation, Chloe threw herself into his waiting arms with all the power of her love carrying her. Kaleb stumbled back a step, wrapping both arms around Chloe's back as she slung her legs around his waist. Asana closed the door, trying to control her anxiety and giving the young couple at least one peaceful moment together before all hell broke loose. Though her mind was full of fear over the consequences of the choice she'd just made in coming to Chloe without Lucias, the sight of her and Kaleb together, of the love that was evident between them, increased the hope she'd only just found again, after centuries of despair, when she first met Chloe.

Seeing a single tear slip down Kaleb's cheek as he continued to hold on to Chloe for dear life, Asana couldn't hold back her own. Her thoughts turned to her daughter, to Anna, who Chloe reminded her of and she hadn't seen for so very long. She often wondered if Anna knew any sort of happiness or love living under Lucias's thumb, and if she was even really still alive.

"I'm so sorry," Kaleb said against Chloe's hair, as he loosened his grip on her and lowered her to the ground. "I've never been as afraid as I was, knowing what that evil bitch had planned. I had to see you, had to know you were okay. I don't care what my father does to me so long as you're safe."

"Oh no, Kaleb; I, I killed her and Lucias will kill you!" Chloe said stepping back from him and shaking her head as the memory of what she'd done rushed back, accompanied by the fear of what Lucias would do to his son if he found him with her.

"She's not dead, Chloe," Asana said from where she sat on Chloe's bed, her eyes fixed on the blood covering the floor. "You gave her your blood, yes?"

Chloe nodded when Asana looked up. "Then you have ended her life as a human, but you have given her another in its place."

"I don't understand; I didn't think it was possible to turn a human."

"It's not; or at least it wasn't, before you," Kaleb responded, stroking Chloe's cheek with his thumb as he stepped closer to her again. "But that's why she's not here; my father took her to feed, to complete her transformation. It's strange; it was something he had promised her even though he knew it could not be done. Now it seems he has kept his word, thanks to you."

"Do you know what this means?" Chloe said, her lip quivering slightly as the reality of what she could do began to sink in. "Lucias will have an unlimited supply of soldiers now."

"It is a blessing, Chloe. I have seen it. So long as you are not mated, you will have this power," Asana added.

"How is that a blessing? He'll keep me locked up here turning humans for the rest of my life and if I don't, he'll kill everyone I care about!"

"But don't you see? Now he can't force you to be his mate." Kaleb said, gripping her chin to turn her face to him as his eyes dropped to her lips. Chloe felt her stomach tighten under the intense gaze of his hooded eyes. She didn't need to be a telepath to understand that it was desire clouding them.

"It means he won't allow me to be anyone's mate," she whispered as he leaned closer, stopping just before their lips touched.

"But it gives us time," he replied, his lips barely grazing hers with each word. Unable to stand it anymore, Chloe pushed up on her toes and pressed her lips against his. Kaleb let Chloe set the pace, so the kiss was gentle, tentative, as she explored the new sensation. Kaleb growled when her tongue darted out and swept across the seam of his lips, but he still held back, remaining conscious of Asana's presence and not wanting to push Chloe. After years of serving his father, Kaleb was not well practiced in gentleness and restraint, but he would learn for Chloe.

Using more willpower than he realized he possessed, Kaleb broke the kiss, despite every cell in his body screaming for him to push it further. "We all knew you would be more powerful than any who came before you, that you would change the world; I just didn't know how much you would change me," he whispered, looking into Chloe's hazy eyes.

She smiled demurely and her eyes fell to his lips again. She wanted more. More time, more kisses, more everything with Kaleb, but Asana's thoughts came pushing in, reminding her of the danger looming over them all.

Lucias will return soon. Kaleb can't be here when he does and I must go to him first, to tell him of my vision of how your mating will destroy your ability to turn humans into our kind. I will leave it to Kaleb to share what else I saw; he knows the story well, but you must not let him linger.

Chloe nodded, still wrapped in Kaleb's arms and in a blur, Asana was gone. Chloe watched as the door closed and her eyes went to the camera mounted in the corner above it.

"Kaleb, what about the surveillance?" she asked in a panic as she tried to step out of his arms. "Lucias is bound to go back through the footage to see what happened with Molly. He'll want to know everything about how it happened and then he'll see you here."

Kaleb held on to her and pulled her close again. "I took care of it. Before we came I disabled the feed to the cameras in this wing. Our kind has had to learn how to cover our tracks over the years through many changes in technology," he responded, reaching up to twist a strand of her hair around his finger. Seeing the worried expression on her face, he continued, "Don't worry; he won't know it was me and I'm guessing he'll be too distracted with his latest discovery to care. The footage he wants is still there."

"You can't stay," she said, satisfied with his response, but still worried.

"I know. I just want to hold you for one more minute, okay?"

Chloe responded by laying her head on his chest and relaxing against him. They stayed that way, neither of them talking or thinking of anything except how good they felt in each other's arms. When their time was up, Kaleb reluctantly released his hold on Chloe, pressed a chaste kiss to her forehead, and walked to the door.

"Wait; Asana said you would share something else she saw."

"Another time," he said, looking back with his eyes full of joy and a bit of sorrow. "Don't worry; it is something very good and I will do everything I can to make sure it comes to pass."

With that, he disappeared through the door before Chloe could so much as sneak a peek into his mind. She put her hands on her hips, frowning as she scanned for Kaleb's stream of consciousness. It was easy enough to find him but, unlike normal, he was resisting her. She wanted to be cross, but they both knew she could gain access if she really wanted to, and she could sense his playfulness in keeping this little secret. It was a side of him she had seen very little of, but she wanted to see more. Having traversed the deepest corners of his mind, sharing his darkest memories, Chloe knew all too well the horrors of Kaleb's life and she was utterly amazed by the good, the strong light of who he truly was, that he'd manage to hold on to in spite of the darkness that had surrounded him from the day he was born. It's easy to be a good person, or at least to behave like one when you've known nothing but love and kindness in your life, but to have your character tested every single day, to fail more often than you've succeeded to fight the darkness, yet somehow keep trying to hold on to the light, that is true goodness, and that was why Chloe fell in love with a man she'd never even touched.

"Asana, what a lovely surprise; though I can probably guess why you're here," Lucias said as he moved out of his playroom into the hallway where she was waiting. He ran a hand through his freshly-washed hair, the smell of soap mixing with the lingering traces of blood and sex to create his overall scent. Asana schooled her features to hide her disgust; a skill she'd mastered over the years. Lucias's mood was more cheerful than she had ever seen, which made her all the more nervous about what she had to tell him.

"Thank you, Sire. As you instructed, I came as soon as I saw something. It's about Chloe, and your human, Molly."

"Yes; shall we continue this discussion in my office?" he said, gesturing in that direction. In a matter of seconds, Asana was seated in one of the chairs across from his desk. "Please continue."

"Of course, Sire. I believe Chloe can do the impossible. I have seen her turn a human into one of us; more specifically, I saw her turn Molly into a vampire. So long as—"

"And when exactly did you see this?" Lucias interrupted.

"Not long ago, Sire. I came searching for you as soon as I recovered." Of course that was a lie, but it was true that her visions were often a great physical strain; at times so much so, that she would pass out.

"I must admit I'm disappointed, for this is information I already possess. Molly's transformation is complete; I have seen," he said smirking as he raised his fingers to his nose," and touched the magnificent creature she has become. Nonetheless, I am pleased. This is far beyond my wildest imagination of the girl's power. I am eager to learn how her blood will change me once we are mated. I believe the time has come at last."

Asana shifted nervously, attempting to prepare for the wrath she was

106

certain to incur for delivering bad news. "Sire, I'm sorry; but there was more to my vision. Chloe's power, this ability to transform humans, it is based in her blood. If she completes the mate bond, the power will be destroyed."

In a blur, Lucias was directly in front of her, his eyes full of rage as he leaned over her. "Tell me exactly what you saw. Do not leave out a single detail," he demanded with a hiss.

"I, I saw Chloe with the red ribbon on her wrist, it was a mating ceremony, and then I saw her with another human on the verge of death, she gave the man her blood, just like Molly, but he died. And then there was another, a woman, who was healthy as far as I could tell and she drank from Chloe's wrist, but did not change either. But then I saw a battle; we were gathered before The Elite, your army as it is now and hundreds more, humans turned by Chloe, still unmated."

"So if I take Chloe as my mate, I must give up what is perhaps her greatest power? And you're certain there was a mating ceremony in the first vision?" Lucias questioned suspiciously, knowing he'd never intended to have one. It was a stupid ritual he didn't believe in, all he believed in was blood. It was what joined them together and what would give him the power he craved.

Asana immediately realized her mistake. "Yes, Sire; your mating ceremony with Chloe. It is not surprising that she would want to say the words; I believe she will come to love you and women need such reassurances. It would be merciful for a man such as you to make the concession for her sake," she lied.

"Yes, I suppose that is possible," he replied, attempting to sound magnanimous, though Chloe was far more powerful than he could ever hope to be, even by siphoning as much of her power as drinking her blood could provide. Lucias paced for a few moments while Asana waited in silence, barely breathing. "I must admit I'm somewhat disappointed," he said, settling into the seat behind his desk. He gathered his hands in front of his face, the fingertips of each touching and pointing up, and closed his eyes.

"No matter, with an army of turned humans to serve me I will easily defeat The Elite and anyone else who dares stand in my way. When I have enough of them and my enemies are destroyed, I will take Chloe," he said, jumping up, his mood once again oddly cheerful. "You may go," he said, dismissively flicking his hand in Asana's general direction.

Asana didn't hesitate, relieved to get away from Lucias's imposing presence as she sped off to her quarters.

CHAPTER 9 - *Love Renewed*

"Open it," Commander Claesson ordered with an edge of relief to his tone. Several hours had passed since the perpetrators of the containment unit break-in were discovered and The Elite leader and team of scientists had witnessed something of a miracle amongst their kind. They'd run countless blood tests on both Ethan and Alexa, finding them both completely free of Lucias's virus.

Dante and Layla were another story. The Commander moved his eyes to them and shook his head. The pair was sprawled out on the floor, still naked, and passed out. With the ferocity of their feeding on one another, Claesson decided to err on the side of caution and provided them with enough bagged blood to drink themselves into unconsciousness. They were essentially blood-drunk, a state which would allow Dante to complete the transformation safely. Unfortunately, with the amount of blood they'd consumed, The

Elite's stores, which were already strictly rationed due to the visiting soldiers, were seriously depleted. Claesson knew he couldn't risk letting the supply run too low due to the possibility of open battle with Lucias that was constantly looming over their heads; so, as much as he hated it, he would contact Davies, a man he'd rather throw in a cell than do any sort of business with.

It wasn't like the black market blood dealer operating out of Boston was any worse than his counterparts around the world, but the fact that he was the Commander's brother-in-law somehow made his offenses seem more egregious. To say the man's methods were questionable was an understatement, but going through traditional channels would require time he didn't have and Davies could deliver quickly.

"I've sent the soldiers outside back to their quarters and your families have been notified; but under the circumstances, they've agreed to hold off on the family reunion until the morning," Claesson stated, turning his attention back to Ethan and Alexa as they exited the cell. He'd been rather busy while the couple was undergoing their testing, speaking with the High Commander and Ethan's family, debriefing the guard and Jester, neither of whom he fully believed about how the earlier events had come to pass; but considering what was at stake, he'd decided not to press the issue for the time being.

"Martinez, you're dismissed, but we're going over all of this again when things settle down. Understand?" The Commander said to the nervous soldier who'd remained in the room to recover from the tranquilizer and to undergo a couple of precautionary blood tests to rule out the possibility of infection. Relieved, Martinez headed for the door. "And make sure you tell Rachel that I need to hear what happened from her, too."

The soldier looked back, his expression puzzled as the Commander raised his eyebrows and inclined his head to the door. Realization dawned and Martinez smiled, speeding off to find his mate. Perhaps Claesson wasn't as much of a hard-ass as they all thought. Protocol required Rachel to be debriefed separately, before contact with anyone, including her husband, but the ancient vampire was giving them the opportunity to get their stories straight, so to speak.

The click of the door closing was barely audible against the loud pounding of Ethan's heart. Alexa pulled him further into the room, their hands having remained joined the entire walk to her room. The couple had remained silent the whole way, walking at what was a natural human pace, just staring at one another.

She pulled his hand up to her face, gently kissing each knuckle as she continued to stare up into his eyes. "I've. Missed. You. So. Much," she whispered, each word separated by a kiss.

Ethan slipped his other hand into her chestnut hair and drew her close, his eyes locked on her full lips. "I've missed you more than I can say, Amor," he whispered against her lips, not quite touching them. A shiver traveled down her spine as his warm breath brushed over her skin. He closed the distance between them, capturing her mouth in a kiss that said everything his words could not. It was gentle, reverent, yet hungry and full of promises of what was to come. Alexa slid her arms around his waist, her hands moving slowly, tracing every chiseled line, committing them to memory. His body felt different, bigger, no doubt a side effect of being infected. If it was possible, it made him even sexier.

His tongue swiped across the seam of her lips, parting them before it plunged into her mouth, tangling with hers and stealing her breath. He was claiming her. Though they'd renewed their blood bond, he needed more; he needed to possess her, to erase everything that had happened, to erase everything he'd done.

Alexa felt the dark turn in his thoughts; felt his guilt rising and pulled back. "Ethan, you have to let it all go. What happened between us before, it was beyond your control. I chose it; you know that, so please forgive yourself. I'm here now, with you, and I'll never leave you again. I promise."

Tears welled up in Ethan's eyes as he stood in awe of the woman he loved, but there was still something he couldn't let go. "I should have trusted in your strength; you tried to tell me. I should have trusted you to make the right choice even when I couldn't." Thinking of his choices brought more pain and regret to the front of his mind. Even though deep down he knew it wasn't his choice, he couldn't stop blaming himself. "Alexa, I must tell you something," he swallowed hard, trying to choke back his pain, "something I did after you were gone. I didn't want to, but…"

"Shh," she whispered placing a finger over his lips, "you don't have to say anything about it. I already know; I knew when it happened." Ethan cringed. "Stop; it's fine, I understand. I could always feel you and I know how much it hurt you even though you thought I was dead. It was Lucias; the infection. It wasn't you. You have to know that, despite everything that has happened, I wouldn't change any of it because it was the price of having you and Chloe. I'd go through all of it again for a life with you."

Alexa relaxed her shields, letting Ethan feel more of her emotions so he would know she truly meant what she was saying. While it had been one of the most painful experiences of her life, she didn't blame Ethan, she couldn't and she knew that the other woman didn't mean anything to him.

Ethan pulled her into his arms and squeezed her so tightly it probably would have hurt if she was still human. Though it was true she did forgive him, thinking about Ethan with that other woman raised something in her; something primal. Alexa pushed against Ethan's arms, forcing him to loosen his grip on her and grabbed his face, yanking his mouth down to hers. She needed to claim him as much as, perhaps more than, he needed to claim her. She needed to imprint herself on every inch of his body, to remove every trace of the other woman and replace it with something new.

Without breaking their kiss, she gripped the neck of his plain gray t-shirt and tore it completely off. Ethan could feel what she wanted, what she needed. He needed it, too. He scooped her up, placing his arm under her ass, encouraging her to wrap her legs around him as he walked them across the room, away from the bed.

Alexa looked at him, her eyes burning with desire, literally glowing as her expression became one of confusion. Ethan growled, still not accustomed to this new side of her which he found unbelievably sexy. "Where are we going?" she asked, licking along the edge of his jaw to his neck. Her eyes fixed on the slow steady strum of his pulse there, her fangs punching through in response. She put her hand up to cover them, still not entirely comfortable with all of the changes to her body, especially the involuntary ones.

"To the bathroom," he husked, looking at her with a puzzled expression. "Why are you covering your mouth?"

"I'm still not used to it, I guess. I feel embarrassed," she replied, lowering her hand as she lifted her lip to reveal the twin points.

"That is so fucking sexy," he practically grunted out as he crushed his mouth against hers and pushed her back into the wall. He scraped his tongue over each fang; careful not to draw blood, knowing if that happened they'd never get to the bathroom. "You don't ever need to hide from me, especially not this," he said, pulling back and gazing at her, his eyes hooded and glowing with desire. "Okay," Alexa replied as she rocked her hips against him while he tried to regain some sort of focus and open the door. "I need a shower; would you wash me?" He finally managed when she paused in the devious motion of her hips, which seemed only to serve to wipe his mind clear of all rational thought.

Alexa moaned; it was exactly what she needed and she loved him all the more for understanding that. "Every inch of you," she whispered and slanted her mouth over his again.

With the door finally open, they made their way to the shower and Ethan fumbled to turn it on without breaking their kiss. Growing impatient, Alexa pulled away and yanked her teal tank top over her head. Seeing it come off like that, Ethan smiled. "That's the same shirt you wore when we traveled to Eleuthera."

"I've been wearing it since I got here. They found our luggage when they were looking for us and one of the investigators was thoughtful enough to return it. It gave me comfort; reminded me of one of the happiest times of my life."

Ethan could feel the warmth of the shower filling the room and lowered Alexa to the floor. He was slow unbuttoning his jeans as he stared into Alexa's eyes, his own full of adoration and desire. Despite everything that was happening around her, everything that had happened, Alexa held on to the good memories. Looking into her eyes, he saw the best version of himself reflected back at him. Alexa mimicked him, working on the button of her shorts before they dropped to the floor to join his pants. Taking in his fully-hard cock, she licked her lips and reached for the sides of her thong, but Ethan beat her to it, gripping the lacy material and ripping it away as he crushed his mouth to hers.

He gripped her ass tightly and hoisted her up again, sliding her heat up the length of his shaft as she held on to him and they moved under the hot spray of water. Alexa tossed her head back, letting the water flow over her face and down her breasts to pool between their joined bodies. Ethan groaned as he followed the flow of water over her face and down to her beautiful mounds with their dusky pink nipples calling to his mouth. Unable to resist, he lowered his head and captured one between his teeth, flicking his tongue over the pert nub. Alexa groaned low in her throat and ground her hips against his erection in response, adding her own moisture to the water already covering him.

He released her nipple with a pop and stared at her again, remaining motionless as he watched her. He wanted nothing more than to lift her up and plunge her down over his hard cock, but he stayed still, waiting for her to look at him. She finally did and he growled again at seeing her eyes. "You are so beautiful," he husked, lowering her to the floor, gritting his teeth at the feeling of her soft body sliding down him. "I remember a promise of having every inch of my body washed," he said, stroking her sides. As much as he wanted to be inside her, to make love to her until he could no longer move, he knew they both needed this small ritual first. It was a gesture of starting fresh, erasing the past so they could face the inevitable challenges of their future with love and strength, completely united.

"I suppose I did," she replied, spinning to grab a red loofa and Ethan's body wash. He smiled when he saw the familiar bottle and looked around the room for the first time, noticing all of his things commingled with hers. She'd set it all up as if he'd been with her all along.

She worked up a good lather with her hands, and then moved meticulously slowly as she carefully washed Ethan from the top of his head to his feet. It was all she could do to stick to the task at hand as her fingers traveled over every sculpted inch of his powerful body. She didn't mention it because she wasn't sure what kind of feelings the changes would bring up for him, but in addition to being broader, which was even more evident without his clothes, Ethan was at least two inches taller. Even in a room designed with the typically large Elite soldier in mind, Ethan was too tall to stand directly under the nozzle and had to crouch for Alexa to wash and rinse his hair.

Alexa stopped and moved back, pretending to survey her work when in reality she just wanted to take a moment to admire the masculine beauty of her mate. Ethan took the opportunity to do the same, biting his lip and flashing some serious fang as his gaze fell to the small thatch of curls between her shapely thighs.

"I think my work here is d—"

Alexa squealed as Ethan stopped her mid-statement by grabbing under her thighs and hoisting her up to balance against the wall, a feat which made her grateful for the high ceilings, while he slipped her legs over his shoulders. He looked up at her and grinned, his expression so sexy she was afraid she would come before he even touched her. Ethan swiped his tongue up the length of her tender flesh and sucked her already-swollen clit into his mouth, making her cry out with pleasure.

As much as she wanted to close her eyes and focus on the sensation of Ethan's skilled tongue working over her delicate skin, she couldn't pull her eyes from the view of him looking up at her with water spraying sideways behind him and running down her trembling legs. Unable to hold on any longer, Alexa gave in and let her head fall back against the wall. The waves of a climax were building quickly, but just before they reached their peak, Ethan stopped and growled low as he turned and licked the inside of Alexa's thigh. Her eyes popped open and she fisted her hands in his hair as she pulled him towards her again, desperate for release, but he resisted and licked her thigh again.

"Ethan, please; don't stop," she moaned, urging him back to her core with her hands.

"I want to try something; I want to taste you here," he husked with another lick up the inside of her thigh. Alexa's fangs dropped lower when she realized what he was asking. "Oh, God; yes, do it!" she moaned, feeling ready to explode with the thought.

He didn't need any more encouragement. He shifted her leg over onto his shoulder to get better access then placed his mouth over the spot, but didn't bite down. He continued to tease the skin with his tongue, pushing lightly with his fangs, building her anticipation and his own. Alexa squirmed beneath his ministrations, trying to push him to pierce her flesh, but he resisted for a moment longer before finally pressing down. The instant his fangs pierced her skin, Alexa came apart and the climax only grew with each gentle pull on the intimate vein, her body trembling so hard it was a miracle he didn't drop her. Ethan slid his fangs from her skin and swiped his tongue over the punctures and Alexa's orgasm finally topped off and ebbed as he lowered her down the front of his body. He held her tight against him with the tip of his steel-hard cock resting against her warm aching flesh. Despite the earth-shattering orgasm she'd just experienced, Alexa needed Ethan inside her like she needed her next breath. She tilted her hips back and forth, rubbing her moisture on his crown as she wrapped her arms around his neck. She inclined her head and tongued his carotid as she tried to push her hips down further, but he held her up even though he was practically vibrating with need for her. He tilted his head, giving her better access to his neck and she couldn't resist, quickly sinking her fangs and pulling hard on his artery. He growled out, finally lessening his hold and letting her body sink down over the head of his cock. With each pull on his vein, he inched her further down over his shaft. When he was finally buried to the hilt, Alexa reared back, releasing his neck as another orgasm rushed over her and her pussy clenched around him like a fist. Ethan watched in awe as Alexa fell apart in his arms, her fangs flashing and a stray drop of his blood dripping down her chin and onto her breast. He leaned down and licked it up before pulling her head forward and devouring her mouth as he moved inside her with slow deliberate strokes.

When the last tremors of her climax subsided, Alexa broke their kiss. Ethan gritted his teeth as he struggled to stop moving. "I want to move," Alexa said, licking over the marks she'd left in his neck. "Put me down," she whispered and he immediately obeyed. Alexa put her hand on his chest and moved him back a step so she could turn around. Ethan's heart nearly jumped from his chest as he took in Alexa's heart-shaped ass while she bent over in front of him and put her arms up on the wall. She looked over her shoulder and him and grinned mischievously. "What are you waiting for?" she asked, swaying her hips from side to side. His cock jumped in response before he grabbed her hips and pushed inside her in one motion until he was completely buried. Alexa cried out, the sensation of him filling her from that angle both pleasurable and a little painful. Apparently, something else had grown as well.

Ethan held her hips tight as he rocked into her again and again, pushing her toward another climax as his own quickly approached. Knowing he couldn't hold on much longer, he let go of Alexa's hips and slid his hand around her waist and between her legs. He moved his finger in slow circles, applying the perfect amount of pressure as his cock slid in and out of her and she found yet another release. Her walls clenched around him, and Ethan lost the battle and tumbled over the edge, his cock pulsing inside of her as her body continued to squeeze him.

Alexa sagged against the wall, her breathing ragged as Ethan slipped from inside her. She'd forgotten that the water, which had mainly been hitting Ethan's back, was still running until it stopped. Ethan placed a towel over her shoulders and pulled her back. She lifted her arms and he proceeded to wrap it around her body, tucking the end on her side to hold it in place. She turned and reached around him to grab the other towel, slinging it around him and catching the end on the other side of his ass. She looked down at his length, still at half-mast, before she covered it with the towel and tucked the end at his hip, securing it the same way he'd done with hers.

Ethan smiled down at her, then moved in a blur and scooped her up in his arms with one arm under her knees and the other behind her back. He kicked open the other side of the double door to make room and carried her out of the shower and to the bed where he set her down on her feet. "Thank you," he said, pulling her to him and kissing her forehead. "Thank you for loving me, for saving me, for being the most incredible woman I've ever known."

Alexa didn't respond, she couldn't over the lump in her throat, but Ethan could feel her reply through their bond and the gentle kiss she stood on her tiptoes to give him.

Ethan tugged his towel and let it drop to the floor before doing the same with hers. "I just want to lay here and hold you with nothing separating us, está bien?" he asked.

She replied by pulling back the sheet and crawling into the bed, holding it up in invitation for him to join her.

"I can't believe it; he's really going to let this slide, isn't he?" Cami said, looking to Martinez, then Rachel. After leaving the Commander, Martinez had gone immediately to his quarters, finding Cami, Jared, and Jasmine waiting there with his wife.

"I think so, if we stick to the story," Martinez replied, squeezing Rachel a little tighter while he rested his hand over her stomach. Though he'd understood they were only trying to protect him, he'd been pretty irate about what they'd done to Rachel. All of that dissipated when she whispered in his ear and told him they were expecting. His friends did what needed to be done to keep his family together, no matter what they decided to do when the baby came.

"I just wish we knew what's going to happen to Dante," he continued with a touch of sadness.

"I knew we shouldn't have let him in there," Cami said, starting to pace.

"There was no keeping him away; he made his choice and there isn't one of us in here who wouldn't have done the same for our mate," Jared replied. There was no arguing that point.

"Jared's right," Jasmine chimed in. "I don't think even the full force of my ability could have persuaded him to stay away. I can't say I really understand it, but all of you mated folks act pretty crazy for each other under the calmest of circumstances," she teased.

"No doubt," Martinez said, nuzzling Rachel's neck for a moment. "But even if everything works out and they find a cure, there's no way the Commander can let Dante skate. He's Elite and he disobeyed a direct order, with plenty of witnesses who know it. The fact that he did it to help a friend or because he's in love won't slide, so he's either heading down South for God knows how many years, or he's out," Martinez added with frustration.

"Heading down South?" Jared asked, looking at Cami, whose expression turned guilty for a moment before she glared at Martinez. Jared knew the soldiers could be punished for their disobedience, but he assumed it would be in the form of crappy assignments on the compound or extra training.

"Oh, shit, sorry. I thought he knew."

Jared zeroed in on Cami and pulled her into his arms. When she wouldn't look at him, he put his fingers under her chin, but she still resisted as she spoke. "I'm sorry I didn't tell you, but it wouldn't have changed anything and I didn't want you to worry."

"Okay, so tell me now," Jared pressed.

"This kind of disobedience, if substantiated," she added to stress that it probably wouldn't happen to her, "is typically punished with a mandatory term at the compound in Antarctica."

"So we would have to live in the South Pole for a while?"

"Not exactly. I would have to go alone."

"For how long?"

"I was there for five years the last time."

"Five years? What the hell did you do?" Jared asked, his tone growing angry.

"I went out on a mission when I was ordered to stay on the compound, but it was a stupid order because the Commander is a chauvinist!"

"Jesus, Cami! Five years for that? What were you thinking? We could have done this without you, to keep you safe!" Jared yelled.

"No, you fucking couldn't because someone who wouldn't raise suspicion had to distract the guard and we couldn't risk telling anyone else. I had to do it, Jared. Ethan's my brother and Alexa's your sister and Chloe is our niece. I couldn't just sit back and let them go it alone just so I could keep my job."

"Wait; what do you mean?"

"Instead of doing my time down South, I could leave The Elite, forever."

"You would do that? For me?" Jared asked, stepping closer and taking Cami's hand.

"It wasn't even a choice, Jared. I can't lose you."

Jared wrapped his arms around Cami and held her tight. Being Elite was everything to her; the fact that she was willing to give it up for him meant more than he could ever say. "I love you," he whispered, kissing her hair. Cami glanced awkwardly at Rachel and Martinez who were watching with surprise and curiosity, then at Jasmine whose expression was almost sad.

"I love you, too," she replied, pinning Martinez with a stare, daring him to say something; a challenge he apparently couldn't resist.

"Well, damn, Jared. It appears you've assisted in freezing hell over, or making pigs fly, or some shit like that," he teased, ducking behind Rachel playfully.

"Fuck you, Martinez," Cami replied, feigning anger. She wasn't pissed; how could she be? She'd never been happier in her life and, after seeing everything her brother and Alexa had endured for their love, she was grateful.

Alexa had only been sleeping for a couple of hours when she bolted up in bed with the feeling you get when waking up from a terrible nightmare that you can't quite remember.

"I'm sorry, Amor. I didn't mean to wake you," Ethan said, already sitting up beside her. She couldn't remember the dream because it wasn't hers. She'd been feeling Ethan through their bond.

"What is it, Ethan?" Alexa asked, though she already knew. She was a mother, after all.

"I think I could find my way back to Lucias's facility. I know he took Chloe there."

"And what would we do if we found it? He has an entire army protecting him."

"I know, yo sé, but we can't just leave her there. Alexa, I watched her go with him. I just stood there; I couldn't even speak as he snatched her away from us."

"Ethan, my love, please listen to me. Chloe is strong, she's so much stronger than you can imagine. She got the best of both of us and more. Going with Lucias was her choice." Alexa took his hand. "I want to try something. I need you to lower your shields as much as you can. My ability isn't as strong as Chloe's but I think maybe with you, because of our bond, I can show you my mind if I focus."

Ethan did as she asked, leaning back against the headboard as he relaxed and focused on opening his mind to her. Meanwhile, Alexa concentrated on the images from Chloe's vision that she'd shared and pushed into Ethan's mind. Scenes passed of Ethan returning to the compound, of them renewing their blood bond in the cell, of what would have happened if Chloe hadn't gone with Lucias.

"We have to trust her and her choices. She sacrificed to save us and it's up to us to make sure it wasn't in vain. The Elite are preparing; your sister is making damn sure of it. They are training around the clock and every available soldier from the other compounds has made their way here to help in the fight. When they are ready, we will go for Chloe, if Lucias doesn't bring the fight here first; but until then, there's nothing we can do."

It was a hard pill to swallow, but Ethan knew that Alexa was right and that it went against every instinct she had as well.

"For now, we need rest. I can feel how exhausted you are. Tomorrow, we'll see our families and talk to your mother. Perhaps she can use her ability to provide some insight. Okay?"

Ethan nodded reluctantly and settled back into bed while Alexa snuggled against him.

CHAPTER 10 - *The Price of Defiance*

Chloe cringed, sensing Lucias's approach. As much as she despised being a part of his darkness, she reached for his mind. She let out a small sigh of relief when she found his thoughts focused on her newfound ability and his discussion with Asana, which ensured that he wouldn't try to complete the mate bond with her. She was just about to pull out of the abyss when images of her and Molly with him, which made her skin crawl, flashed before her. She started to panic; her mind reeling as she tried to find a way to escape such a fate without incurring Lucias's wrath. It seemed that Asana's vision would keep him from making her his mate, but completing a blood bond and sex were two completely different things. It stood to reason that the power in her blood would be unaffected if Lucias were to try and engage in the other unsavory activities always at the front of his mind.

She considered calling to Kaleb, but if he knew her fear, he would come to her and try to challenge his father; a fight he couldn't win and that would probably cost him his life. Instead she searched for Asana, but before she could pinpoint her stream of consciousness, the door swung open.

Lucias ran his gaze up the length of her well-covered body, his eyes and mind full of devious intent until he took a step into the room. In an instant, his eyes clouded over with rage. As quickly as he'd appeared, Lucias was gone. Chloe remained stock still, grateful, but confused as she tried to understand what had just happened. She focused on Lucias, trying to find the answers in his mind, but it was impossible to decipher the source of his rage through the red cloud surrounding it. She looked around her room, wondering if there was something there that could have set him off. Then it dawned on her. She inhaled deeply, her hand shooting up over her mouth the instant she knew.

Kaleb and Asana had been certain to cover their tracks by disabling the security footage, but they hadn't considered masking their scents, which among vampire kind were as unique and identifying as fingerprints were to humans.

Chloe sped around the room, growing hysterical as she thought of what Lucias might do to them and wondering why he hadn't said anything to her. She knew the answer; he feared her as much as he desired to possess her despite the threats he used to keep her under control. He knew she would do his bidding to keep her family safe, but as much as he tried to conceal it, he was afraid that one day she would call his bluff if he pushed her too far.

She tried to calm down enough to focus and warn Kaleb and Asana before Lucias reached them, even though she knew it wouldn't do them much good. Like her, he controlled Asana with what she loved, her daughter Anna. Kaleb he controlled through his sire bond and the threat of infection. Asana was too valuable for him to hurt her, but Kaleb was another story. He was his son, but Lucias had resented him since the day he was born.

Finding it impossible to focus, Chloe threw open the door and sped out after Lucias, not knowing what she would do, but determined to do whatever she could to protect her new friend and the man she loved.

Asana fell back on the bed as a new vision overtook her. A tear slid down her cheek as Anna's face came into focus. She was alive. It had been so long since she'd seen her that she was afraid she'd forgotten what she looked like. The joy was brief as the scene shifted to reveal Lucias standing over her, his eyes locked on Asana as he plunged a needle into Anna's heart. The images began to blur, an indication that the vision was coming to an end, but Asana struggled to hold on, needing to know more. Anna looked her way, her eyes glowing red, and then she disappeared. The vision had been short; not enough to deplete Asana's strength like so often happened, but what it revealed took more than her strength as her body was racked with sobs so hard that the bed shook beneath her.

Chloe? she called out in her mind, knowing that the powerful vampire was the reason her daughter was in danger and the only hope of saving her. It had been Asana's choice; even without the insight of her visions to guide her, she'd known when Kaleb asked that it was a great risk to go to Chloe in her room. She'd felt it in her bones, but she went anyway, understanding that Chloe needed them. The sweet young vampire was the key to it all; Asana had been certain of that for centuries and, despite all she had lost and suffered, she held on to the hope that, in the end, Chloe would bring peace to their kind.

"Asana, you disappoint me," Lucias said from the doorway, his voice eerily calm. Asana shot up and immediately fell to her knees, lowering her head in a final desperate act of submission that she hoped would somehow appease him. He knew she'd gone to Chloe; it was the only explanation for her vision. He would infect Anna to punish her.

"Sire, it was only to serve you," she began, "Chloe is lonely and afraid here. I thought if I went to her, if I shared some of what I'd seen, I could help to guide her towards her destiny of serving by your side as you've always planned."

"I see; and you did not think to discuss this plan with me?"

"You were busy when I had my last vision, the one of Molly's transformation. I know better than to disturb you, Sire, and Chloe was in need of a friend after what had happened; she was vulnerable, scared. It was the perfect time to gain her confidence."

"Indeed," Lucias agreed. In a flash he was before her, his hand wrapped around her throat as he raised her from the ground and suspended her flailing body in the air. "And how did my son fit into this little plan of yours?" he spat vehemently, throwing her against the

130

wall. Asana crumpled to the floor, gasping for air as her bruised windpipe started to heal.

"It seems I have been too lenient with you over the years, Asana. You have forgotten your place. I believe it is high time that you were reminded who it is you serve. Why was my son with you? I suggest you think carefully before you answer me; if I detect the hint of a lie, I will remove your daughter's head and mount it on your wall."

"Then you may as well kill me," Asana said, her voice hoarse but growing stronger as she stood up straight, defiant. "I only serve to keep her safe. If you take her from me you will lose the benefit of having a seer in your employ. You will face your future in the dark."

Lucias sneered and took a step towards her, but she didn't back down. "This is a side of you I have not yet seen. The thought never appealed to me before, but seeing you like this, perhaps you should spend some time with me in my playroom. I do enjoy a good fight."

Even after years of practice, Asana couldn't hide her disgust as bile rose up in her throat. She'd sooner die.

"Perhaps not," Lucias continued, "I think it's time for Anna to visit and we'll see how strong your resolve is then. If you wish to live to see her again, you are not to leave this room until I summon you. It's time for me to spend a little quality time with my son."

When he was gone, Asana fell back to her knees.

Chloe?

Though she could barely hear anything over the pounding of her own heart, Chloe listened intently for Asana's thoughts as she moved through the unfamiliar corridors. She grew bolder with each step and had already incapacitated several of Lucias's infected soldiers posted along the way. Even through her panic, a vision came to Chloe shortly after she left her room. It was only a flash; Lucias's army gathered outside of Boston. She knew it was near the compound, remembering the scenery from her own journey there. Lucias was upset, angry as some of his men approached. In that instant Chloe realized that Lucias couldn't find a way in. He couldn't get to her family; his men couldn't get to her family.

Chloe? She finally heard and stopped. At almost the same moment, she sensed Lucias, but he was moving away; his mind so full of rage that she couldn't make sense of his thoughts, but still somehow more restrained, calculating.

Please, Chloe, where are you? Asana asked again.

I'm here, she replied telepathically. *I think I'm close to your room. Which is it?*

An image of the corridor flashed before Chloe's eyes and focused on a door. She turned to see the same door on the left a few yards away. After a quick look around, she sped over and passed through.

Before the door closed, Asana rushed to her and Chloe wrapped her arms around her trying to offer some small amount of comfort.

"Chloe, you shouldn't be here." *He knows we came to you. I tried to cover by saying that you needed a friend. I had another vision before he came to me.* Asana sent before focusing on the vision, which passed through Chloe's mind in time with Asana's thoughts.

"I was worried about you; I know you broke the rules to come see me. I'm so grateful; you really helped." *I'm so sorry, Asana.* Chloe sent, knowing it was necessary for them to keep certain parts of their conversation silent to avoid Lucias's surveillance. The vision was no news to Chloe since she'd seen it long before Asana had, but had kept to herself. Chloe didn't fully understand why, but something in her gut told her not to tell.

I don't know what to do. He threatened to kill her, but this is almost worse. If he infects her, he can make her do anything he wants. I can't stand to think of it; it would almost be better if she died.

Don't think like that. A cure is possible, I saw it with my father; if it comes to that, we'll find a way to bring her back.

I hope you're right, but there's more, Chloe. He knows Kaleb was with me; he's on his way to him now.

Chloe felt her stomach drop; even though she'd known Kaleb was in danger, it became that much more real when Asana said it. *I know. He detected your scents in my room. I'm going to find him; if I can get to him, I think I could knock him out and we could escape. I had a vision. He can't get to my family now and if we can get to the compound, he won't be able to get to us.*

133

But, Chloe, my daughter! He'll kill her if I leave.

I don't know what else to do, Asana. This could be my only chance.

Asana's eyes darted around as she tried desperately to think of something. *Then you should go. Find Kaleb and go, but knock me out first. Then I can at least try to convince Lucias that I tried to stop you.*

Asana, no—

Before she finished her thought, the door flew open. Both women had been so lost in their conversation that they hadn't noticed Mason's approach.

He looked back and forth between the two women with his red eyes, and smirked. "This makes my job easier. Lucias wants both of you upstairs. Now," he said, holding the door expectantly. Chloe pushed into his mind, surprised to find something she'd never encountered before. The strength of her telepathy typically allowed her to access both current thoughts and memories unless a person's emotional state was abnormally unstable, as in cases of extreme rage or stress. Neither was the case for Mason, but all she could see was the image of herself and Asana in present time. There were no other thoughts, no memories. His mind was like a video camera that didn't record.

"I'm guessing you'll want to hurry," Mason said before flying off down the corridor. The two women looked at each other, their eyes full of fear and unanswered questions, before the sped off after him.

Chloe entered the large room where Lucias was waiting and felt her power rising, threatening to spiral out of control as she looked at Kaleb. He was unconscious, strung up against the far wall, his arms and legs chained, and he was almost completely covered in blood. She clenched her hands into fists at her sides and turned to Lucias.

"I wouldn't be too hasty, my dear. Look around. You are surrounded by my men, and there are ten times as many outside. If anything happens to me, they'll kill my son and Asana. You may be powerful, but you can't take on that many at once."

He was right. The scale of mind blast Chloe would need to take out the men in the room would wipe her out and leave her defenseless against the men outside for more than enough time for them to kill Kaleb and Asana.

"I must say, your presence here seems to have encouraged great change in my son. If only he had been so strong in serving his father and master," Lucias said, casting an almost admiring glance at his only child. "Even under the pain of the sire bond he refused to tell me anything. I doubt the two of you will be so willful." Lucias nodded to the man closest to Kaleb, who then produced a large blade and pressed it to Kaleb's neck hard enough to break the skin and draw fresh blood.

"What do you want?" Chloe yelled, clutching the skirt of her dress.

"Tell me why my son was in your room."

"He came to make sure I was okay after Molly attacked me."

"So he knew of your vision, Asana? I thought as much. What else have you shared with my son? What else have you seen?" Lucias demanded as he sped across the room, stopping only inches from her.

Asana lifted her chin defiantly and remained silent.

"Not feeling talkative? Perhaps this will loosen your tongue," he said with a sneer as he flicked his hand towards one of the doors which was immediately opened. A woman and child were shoved through, both falling to their knees. The girl who appeared to be no older than ten years old was crying as she looked at her mother with eyes full of fear and confusion.

"Anna?" Asana said, as her eyes locked on the woman whose face was downcast and shielded by her long red hair. She raised her gaze and her hair fell away. Asana gasped; her hand shooting up to her mouth as tears filled her eyes.

"Yes, your sweet Anna is all grown up and a mother herself," Lucias said with a great deal of satisfaction. "You see, I am not so cruel. I let your daughter live a fairly normal life; she has a mate, she has children, this daughter and a son who I have left untouched with his father." Asana felt the briefest moment of joy knowing that her sweet Anna had been granted so much mercy, though she suspected Lucias's motives had been more devious than he would let on. Supernatural abilities, like physical traits, were typically genetic. Lucias wanted to continue Asana's line in the hopes of attaining another seer. "They may remain in their home," he continued, "safe and unaware, and I will let Anna and your granddaughter live. It all depends entirely on you and the next words that come out of your mouth. So I ask you again, what have you seen and what does it have to do with my son?" he demanded, pacing the floor in front of Anna and the child.

Asana's eyes shot to Chloe. As much as she wanted to tell her to lie, or keep quiet, she couldn't ask her friend to risk her family, so instead she only nodded to Asana with understanding in her eyes.

"The mating ceremony; it was not with you, it was with Kaleb. They are in love," she whispered, lowering her head.

Lucias stopped and stood perfectly still for a moment. Chloe pushed into his mind and to her surprise found that his rage had dissipated and the tone of his emotions resembled something closer to satisfaction. She soon realized why.

"Is this true, Chloe? Do you love my son? I believe Asana would appreciate sincerity in your response. Her daughter's life depends on it."

Lucias had known it would only be a matter of time before Chloe realized that his control over her was limited. As expected, and confirmed by his source within The Elite who'd managed to smuggle a message to him, the Elite female he'd left behind would be of little use, remaining under lockup in a highly restricted wing of the compound. Without her assistance, or that of another Elite soldier, he couldn't gain entry to the compound and would have to draw the enemy out when the time came. When he realized Asana's defiance, he'd suspected she'd had a vision that revealed that he'd lost his leverage against Chloe, forcing him to act.

Chloe didn't hesitate; there was too much at stake and she now knew Lucias's intentions. Lying would only serve to hurt her friend. "Yes."

Lucias actually smiled. No one knew of his other mate bond, the one to the mole he'd implanted amongst his enemies, but as much as he'd wanted to share in Chloe's power, the fear of breaking that connection had always lingered in the back of his mind. Once a mate bond was completed, no one ever replicated the process; many believed it to be physiologically impossible, so there was no way to know if the previous bond, the one which actually meant something to him, would be eradicated by a new one. Now, with the power of turning humans at stake if Chloe mated, he wouldn't have to find out and he no longer needed the bond to control his powerful little vampire. He had Kaleb for that.

"Then it would serve you well to be compliant to all my future requests, if you wish for him to live," Lucias said, moving towards his son who was starting to awaken. He gestured to one of his soldiers, who produced a large syringe from a nearby table. Lucias remained silent while Kaleb tried to comprehend his surroundings. Seeing Chloe and Asana, he bucked against the chains, but he was still far too weak to break free.

Don't fight him, my love. It will be okay. Everything will be okay. I swear to you. Chloe sent as she cried silently at knowing what was coming. The horror of it flashed in Kaleb's eyes when he saw the syringe. Before the protest manifested on his lips, Lucias plunged the needle into his chest.

"Take him to one of the cells. After a few hours, send in one of the humans Molly procured this morning."

Chloe's gritted her teeth as she fought to control her rage, which threatened to unleash her power on Lucias for his cruelty. He meant for Kaleb to suffer. First by enduring the pain of the infection for hours without the relief of feeding, and then by forcing him to take a human life; something he knew his son tried to avoid, though he never let on to his knowledge of what he perceived to be a great deficiency of character in his child.

Two infected made quick work of Kaleb's chains and whisked him away as instructed, while Chloe watched helplessly.

"Now, what to do about you, Asana? I did say I would let your daughter live, but you have defied me; you must pay some price for that. I cannot abide such disobedience."

Asana fought the urge to cover her eyes as her earlier vision came to life, and Lucias revealed a second syringe and stood over Anna who was still kneeling beside her daughter. Instead, she watched, holding Anna's gaze as her eyes silently pleaded for help Asana couldn't give, as Lucias added her to the ranks of his infected with a single shot.

Asana fell to her knees, as the granddaughter she'd never met screamed and her daughter writhed with the pain of the virus burning through her system.

"When night falls, return the child to her father. Take this one to a cell to complete transformation," Lucias ordered, eyeing Asana and

Chloe.

Asana looked up at him, clearly defeated by what had transpired, which made him smile. "Please, I beg you, let me speak to my granddaughter; let me meet her, just once," she begged.

Lucias's smile broadened and he reached down to grip her chin. "I think not."

CHAPTER 11 - *A New Hope*

Alexa lay awake, having only slept for a few minutes before her conscience got the better of her. She couldn't stop thinking about Dante. Though she knew he probably felt some peace in being with Layla, she still worried for her friend, with Lucias's virus overtaking his body and mind, and she had an idea that she just couldn't shake. She turned to Ethan, seeing his handsome features perfectly in the dark as he slept. She'd felt his exhaustion, which had been a constant in him for the past weeks throughout which he barely slept, even by vampire standards, knowing he would be out for quite a while still. Alexa lifted the arm covering her stomach and slid towards the edge of the bed. Ethan stirred, reaching for her in his sleep, so she moved her pillow under his arm, which he pulled in close to his body and settled. Alexa reached for his mind and smiled, seeing him dreaming of their family all together, happy and content for the first time in what seemed like forever. She hoped the image in his mind was truly in their futures.

Satisfied that he wasn't going to wake, Alexa moved silently through the darkness, gathering her clothes from the floor and getting dressed in seconds before she slipped out the door.

It was still early and, based on the cacophony of thoughts floating about, most of the compound was awake and buzzing about the day's events. Alexa pushed up a layer in her shields to block them out and another to lessen the impact of her bond with Ethan, concerned that he would feel that she was gone or some emotion in her would wake him before she reached her goal. Since becoming a vampire, she'd learned to channel her ability in ways that weren't possible while her true nature was repressed by the witch's spell. Her talent wasn't as powerful or versatile as Chloe's, but she could zero in on certain streams of consciousness without any background thoughts from others nearby and seek a mind from a greater distance.

Moving towards the mind she sought, she felt a small tinge of guilt for what she was doing, knowing that Ethan would be furious, but she had to see Dante and help him if she could. He'd been a great friend to her, a source of comfort and hope when she needed it most; an ally when she fought to save her mate so she couldn't just abandon him. She pushed down her feelings of guilt and pressed on.

Turning into the other residential wing, Alexa was relieved to find the corridor between the rooms, which were occupied mainly by soldiers, empty. Not that she was doing anything wrong, but she preferred to avoid explaining herself to anyone she didn't have to. She focused her telepathy, listening as she moved, trying to find her target since she had no idea which room was his. Fairly confident that she had the right one, she stood at the door and took a deep breath, steeling her nerves before she pressed the button.

She jumped slightly when the door flew open without any response through the intercom. "Alexa, is everything all right?" Commander Claesson asked, his eyes shooting around with the discerning gaze of a soldier with millennia of experience, assessing the area and searching for possible threats.

"Yes, of course; I'm so sorry to disturb you, but could I speak to you for a moment?"

His eyebrows bunched over his eyes for a moment before he sighed and stepped back, gesturing for her to enter. There was a part of him, a rather old fashioned part, that thought to refuse her, simply because a lady shouldn't be in alone in the room of a man who wasn't her husband, but he was finally trying to catch up with the times.

"How can I help you, Alexa?" he queried, closing the door.

"I know this is asking a lot, sir, but please hear me out," she said, pacing nervously as she spoke.

The Commander nodded, indicating that he was willing to listen. "Ethan is cured, that much is sure; because he took my blood."

"Yes, because he's your mate and you were already linked. The doctors think it may have been the preexisting connection that kept the infection from fully invading Ethan's cells, keeping a small part

143

of him free of it."

"Right, but what if they're wrong; what if it's just my blood that cured him?"

The Commander shook his head. "Of course we considered that possibility, but it's not the case. Samples of your blood were combined with some from Dante and Layla with no change."

"I knew that already, but did the virus spread to my cells in the sample?" she asked, almost certain that she was on to something.

The Commander looked at her, obviously intrigued. "I'm not sure."

"Would you take me to the containment unit, to the lab? There's something I want to try?"

"I'm going to need you to be more specific if you expect for me to break the protocols I set, which you've already ignored once today," the Commander replied, giving her a look.

"Of course," she said, stopping in front of him. "When I was in the cell with Ethan, I drank his blood while he was drinking mine. What if I'm immune to the virus, but in order for the immunity in my blood to be shared, I have to drink from the infected?"

The Commander thought for a moment. She could be on to something, but even if she was right, her idea was not without some pretty significant obstacles.

"Even if you're right, how the hell are we supposed to test it? It's too dangerous for you to get close enough to one of them and," he said looking at her pointedly, "I'm venturing a guess that you haven't shared this little idea with your husband, since I doubt he'd let you out of his sight willingly at his point. Not to mention, as a bonded male myself, I know with absolute certainty he'll have to be locked up and probably tranquilized before he'll let you feed from another male."

"That's why we have to go now, while Ethan is still sleeping," Alexa said. "And I do think there's a way for me to get close enough; if I can get through to Dante, maybe I can bite him the same way they draw blood for the test."

"I'm all for putting an end to this damn virus, but I really think you need to talk to your husband about this first. Besides, we can't spare the blood to coerce Dante or Layla to cooperate right now; they've practically cleaned out our stores already. "

"I think I can get Dante to give me his arm without offering blood and you know the saying, it's better to beg for forgiveness than ask for permission. Like you said, there's no way Ethan will let me drink from another man willingly; we have to do this without him knowing. The more time that passes, the harder it will be for me to reach Dante until the virus runs its course. You said yourself it can take weeks or months, in some cases, before the infected starts to resemble who they were before and even then, they're not the same. We don't know what Lucias has planned, but he has my daughter and we're running out of time. If we have to, we can use tranquilizers. It's what Dante would want."

The Commander thought for a moment. He and the High Commander had been doing everything in their power to prepare for the fight ahead; they were on the verge of implementing the human integration protocols, and had a few tricks up their sleeves, but as it stood, defeating Lucias was still a long shot. If they found a cure for the virus, then maybe, just maybe they could take away Lucias's greatest advantage and end the war once and for all.

"You know I'm probably going to end up losing a limb for being a part of this," the Commander teased, though in the back of his mind, he couldn't help but think mutilation was a real possibility when Ethan found out what they were up to. He was, by far, the strongest of their kind; the Commander was well aware of that fact, having spent countless years trying to persuade the elusive vampire to join his ranks.

Alexa smiled, feeling victorious and excited as the Commander acquiesced and headed for the door.

Alexa followed Commander Claesson through the first door to the containment unit where Dante and Layla were still being held. They'd been left in the cell together for the time being because, despite the number of years they'd been researching the virus, there was a lot they didn't know about it and all of its side effects. With Dante being newly infected, they worried what impact the amount of sedative that would be required to knock him out would have on his body.

Per the Commander's request, Dr. Jones and two other members of his team were already right outside the second door. Their excitement was palpable. When he'd called the doctor, Commander Claesson filled him in on Alexa's thoughts about how to activate her immunity in others.

Dr. Jones sped over the instant she stepped through. "Alexa, I'm embarrassed to say we never considered what effect the taking of Ethan's blood while he drank from you may have had. Now that you presented the idea, it makes perfect sense. It's genius really. It's just a theory, but I suspect when you ingest infected blood, it activates your immune response; but given the speed of our metabolisms, the signs of that response were cycled out before we drew your blood for testing."

"I just hope it works," Alexa replied, looking to the Commander who was about to open the main door. "I think I need to go in alone," she said, looking through the small window to the cell where Dante was being held. She couldn't see him, but she could sense his tormented mind. "Just for a few moments to see if I can still reach him; if we all go in, his bloodlust will surely take over."

"Fine, Alexa, but under no circumstances are you to open that cell. We installed a key code panel after your stunt earlier, but don't try to tell me you don't know the code; I know you've been poking around in my head."

She didn't bother trying to deny it; she had pushed into his mind when his shields had been relaxed just enough while she was trying to sell him on the idea of bringing her down to the containment unit. Knowing a person's thoughts can be quite helpful in the art of persuasion. She had no intention of opening the cell; she knew it was too great a risk even though she was probably immune.

She nodded in response. "So we're clear," he continued, removing his sidearm from the holster and pulling the slide, "if you free either of them, as much as I'll hate it, I'll put them down. I can't risk the other lives on this compound, and you shouldn't be willing to, either."

"I understand," Alexa replied.

With that, he stood clear as the door opened and Alexa moved through.

Alexa barely breathed as she moved towards Dante's cell. Though she knew they wouldn't be able to hear her even if she screamed, she crept across the room quietly until she was directly in front of the enclosure. Only the security lights were on in the lab, so the cell was dark, but she could see Dante and Layla perfectly with her preternatural night vision. She reached for the button to make contact with Dante, but jumped back when he suddenly appeared on the other side of the glass; completely naked and only inches away from her with his red eyes glowing bright in the darkness.

There was a fierce hunger and pain in them, but also something else. Recognition.

Alexa she placed her palm against the glass, careful to keep her gaze upwards. Dante's red eyes shot to it, their bright glow reflecting off the glass. He looked back at Alexa, inching closer as he raised his own palm to rest on the barrier directly over hers. A single tear slid down her cheek. Dante was still in there and he still knew her. They were connected.

Their connection was broken when the room practically vibrated from a roar just outside the room. Alexa cringed as the anger swept over her despite the barrier she'd placed to lessen the mate bond. Ethan. He was awake, right outside the door, and a long way beyond pissed off.

Alexa looked over her shoulder, her palm still over Dante's as she saw Ethan's green-gray eyes glowing back at her through the tiny window of the door. She snatched her hand away and sped to the entrance as it slid open. Before words could even register in her mind, Ethan had her in his arms, squeezing her so tightly that she could barely breathe. She was surprised at the sense of relief she felt passing through their connection, but it was short lived as he finally released her and his anger began to seep back in.

"Two things," he began, staring at her with eyes full of intensity, "I'm sorry, I know it's brutish of me, or whatever you want to call it, but you can't leave my sight without telling me where you're going, at least for a while. Second of all, we're leaving. The Commander filled me in on your little plan. No. Fucking. Way." he said, punctuating each word.

"Ethan," Alexa began, putting her hand on his cheek, "if I can help, if my blood can cure him, I have to try."

"Don't you mean them?" Ethan asked, his tone harsh, almost accusing as his eyes moved to Dante's naked form.

149

Guilt flashed in Alexa's eyes and Ethan didn't miss it; that was the trouble with the mate bond. "What is it about him?" he asked, his voice growing louder as he grabbed her wrist and pulled the hand he'd seen pressed again the glass to his own cheek. "Do you have feelings for this male?" he pressed.

"Ethan, no," she started, but then stopped. "Well, yes, but not like that," she insisted, seeing the flames of anger flare higher in Ethan's eyes. "He's my friend; he was there for me when you couldn't be, Ethan." She regretted her choice of words the instant they left her lips and Ethan's anger took a backseat to the pain he felt at hearing a reminder of what he considered his failing the woman he loved.

"My love, I don't blame you; you know that. I just needed comfort, needed a friend," she said, but her mind betrayed her in the worst way, bringing the kiss she shared with Dante to the front of her mind and sending her guilt to new heights.

Ethan looked at her hard, the question in his eyes. Alexa knew she couldn't avoid it, and she couldn't lie to him. Not after everything they'd been through. She took one deep breath, then another, terrified of how Ethan would respond. "We kissed, just once," she whispered.

His jaw clenched so hard she could hear his teeth grating together as his glare shot to Dante, who was watching the entire exchange, the primal hunger of infection again glowing in his eyes. The way he looked, Alexa was afraid Ethan would burst through the glass of the cell just to get to Dante on the other side.

"Ethan, it was innocent. I swear to you, we just understood each other; we were going through the exact same hell. Like I told you earlier, he's in love with Layla," she said, not even sure if Ethan knew the other infected vampire's name. They hadn't talked about her or anything to do with the time he was infected since Ethan had tried to apologize earlier. It had been Alexa who'd stopped him and insisted they leave it in the past and move on, but based on the knot in her stomach, that was about to change.

Ethan's heart started pounding. He'd been so happy just to see and be with Alexa again that he didn't want anything to take away from that, especially after he found out Alexa already knew about and forgave his time with another woman. He wasn't sure if Alexa knew it was Layla or not, but he wasn't going to push his luck by asking.

Based on the way she was acting, he realized that Alexa knew what happened, but she didn't know it was Layla. Before he could stop it, memories of his time with her flashed in his mind. Sensing the dramatic change, and before she could think better of it, Alexa pushed into Ethan's mind.

"I think I'm going to be sick," she groaned, stepping out of Ethan's reach and approaching the cell again where Dante was still standing, staring, and now joined by Layla. "It was her? She's the woman you fucked?!" she screamed, already knowing the answer. The rational part of her mind knew it shouldn't matter, knew it didn't change anything, but when it comes to love, rationale typically flies out the window. It wasn't any different for Alexa as the need to vomit was quickly replaced by a deep unreasonable desire to rip out Layla's throat.

✧

Though he'd tried to stay out of it as long as he could, Commander Claesson decided that it was time to intervene before things got out of hand. He'd only let Ethan into the containment unit because he saw and understood the pain he was feeling and he knew Alexa would be able to calm him down. Besides, if he didn't let him pass he was pretty sure his earlier prediction about losing limbs would have come true. And he hadn't known anything about the dynamic between the foursome inside at the time, but based on the way Alexa had just yelled, the entire compound and most of Boston knew about it now.

"Alexa, maybe it's best we wait on this whole thing for a while. Maybe give you two a little time to talk things over, cool down a bit," Claesson said, trying to diffuse the situation. The emotional temperature of the room was about as intense as any battle or crisis situation he'd ever experienced.

"No. We will do this now," she said, her voice suddenly calm again as she turned and pinned Ethan with her stare, daring him to try to stop her after what she'd just discovered. Ethan clenched his fists at his sides so tightly that his nails cut into his palms, but he remained quiet.

The Commander looked toward Ethan, then back at Alexa and sighed before he opened the door and signal for Dr. Jones and the others to come in.

"Ethan, maybe you should step out for a few minutes," he said gently, knowing it was going to be damn near impossible for Ethan to watch what was about to happen.

"I'm not going anywhere," he growled.

"Suit yourself," Alexa tossed over her shoulder as she moved closer to the cell and stood in front of Dante. Layla eyed her hungrily while Alexa resisted the urge to flip her off. Again, she knew that what had happened was beyond Ethan and Layla's control, but it didn't make it hurt any less and, somehow, the fact that Dante loved Layla made it hurt just a little bit more. That was one bit of information she was sure it was best to keep quiet no matter how angry with Ethan she was.

Pressing the intercom, she began to speak. "Dante, I need for you to let me take your blood," she said quietly. His expression remained virtually unchanged, but the glow in Layla's eyes flared.

Good. Alexa thought to herself, feeling some small, and admittedly petty, sense of satisfaction in getting a rise out of the infected female.

"I can help you and Layla," she continued, pushing into his mind. His thoughts were flooded with bloodlust, but there was a tiny sliver focused on her words. "If you let me feed from you, I will feed you in return."

With lightning speed, he moved to the small opening in the cell used for collecting blood samples. Ethan growled from somewhere behind her, but Alexa ignored him and followed Dante. He pushed his arm through and one of the scientists approached to operate the restraints for Alexa.

"It's safe now; he can't move until we release him," the man said, stepping back to make room for her. She moved closer and started to bend down to Dante's arm, but froze and spun around at seeing his erection. Seeing Ethan's face and the blood running from his clenched fists, she felt guilty for it, but was glad for the ability to block their connection. She couldn't imagine how she would feel if the situation was reversed. Then in her peripheral vision she caught a glimpse of Layla, who was also completely nude, and realized that she knew exactly how he was feeling since she'd essentially witnessed the entire scene when he was with Layla. Still, she loved Ethan too much to take pleasure from his pain; none of this was about them. It was about saving her friend and, ultimately, their daughter.

"Ethan, come here," she whispered, holding out her hand. He looked at her, confused, then relieved, before he made his way across the room to entwine his fingers with hers. She stood up on her tiptoes and pressed a soft kiss on his lips. "I love you, Ethan. Only you, forever," she whispered against his lips.

He pulled back and nodded, squeezing her hand. Keeping her eyes on Ethan, Alexa lowered her mouth to Dante's arm. She smiled up at him with her fangs flashing before she bit down on Dante's wrist. As much as he wanted to close his eyes to avoid seeing it, Ethan held Alexa's gaze. If it had to happen, he was going to be there with her for every second of it. Alexa took two long pulls from Dante's vein and immediately released him.

"Now we'll just take a few vials," Dr. Jones said, stepping over with a needle to draw Alexa's blood. He filled the first vial and passed it to one of the other scientists. The other man immediately transferred Alexa's blood to a syringe and shot it into Dante's forearm which was still restrained. Dr. Jones filled two more vials before flashing to one of the microscopes. "Now we'll just mix this sample with one from patient two, and see what happens."

Everyone in the room seemed to be holding their breath, looking back and forth between Dante and Dr. Jones, waiting for some sort of result.

"Absolutely remarkable," Dr. Jones whispered to himself.

"What is it?" Commander Claesson asked anxiously.

"She was absolutely right; the new samples of Alexa's blood are working. See for yourself," he said, stepping away from the microscope to make room for the Commander.

"Oh, my God," he said at seeing the tiny cells waging war beneath the lens. Within seconds, all evidence of Lucias's virus was gone.

They all looked toward Dante who had sunk to his knees with his hands against the glass and his head bowed. After what felt like an eternity, he looked up at Alexa with familiar and very clear blue eyes.

Alexa squealed and wrapped her arms around Ethan. "We're going to get her back," she whispered, "we're going to get our Chloe back."

Ethan carried an exhausted Alexa back to their room. He kicked the door open and stepped inside while she smiled up at him.

"You know, I can still walk just fine," she teased.

"I know, but you should not have to after what you just did."

"Ha, I just sat there, snacked on some red cells and watched my blood flowing through a tube. I'm more tired from lack of sleep than donating blood; they gave me plenty to replace what they took."

He sat her on the bed, dropped to his knees, and pulled off her shoes. "Then you will rest, but I want to feed you first."

"Ethan, I don't think I can stand the sight of another drop of bagged blood right now," she said, scrunching up her nose. In order to collect her blood while the antiserum was present, the doctor had to continually feed her Layla's infected blood to trigger her immunity.

"I don't want you to drink from a bag," he said pulling his shirt over his head. "I want you to drink from here," he continued, running his finger above his collarbone.

Looking at Ethan's golden skin, Alexa suddenly felt hungry for something, just not blood.

"Maybe if you help me work up an appetite first," she said, licking her lips.

He moved between her legs, his expression serious before he pressed his head against her chest. "Amor, I had to watch you feed from another male. I need for you to take my blood. Please."

Alexa's heart melted. There was nothing like having such a powerful man completely vulnerable and at her mercy. "Oh, Ethan! I'm so sorry, I didn't even think about that. You have to forgive me; after spending a quarter of a century thinking I was just a human, you're going to have to give me some time to get up to speed on vampire etiquette," she teased, trying to ease his mind as she hugged him to her chest and ran her fingers through his hair.

She lifted his face to her and kissed him hard. He crawled up, sliding her back onto the bed as he covered her body with his. He deepened the kiss, stroking his tongue in perfect rhythm with hers, lighting a fire in the pit of her stomach before he rolled to his back and pulled her on top of him.

She sat up and yanked off her top, tossing it aside as she reached for the button on her jeans. Ethan grabbed her hands, as if he intended to stop her. She gazed down at him and smiled softly. "I don't want anything between us when you feed me," she whispered.

She squealed at how fast Ethan moved her, and within seconds they were both completely naked and back in their original positions. "Wow, ask and ye shall receive; I'll have to remember that," she said jokingly, her tone growing more serious with each word as her gaze moved down Ethan's sculpted torso to the hardness laying against him reaching almost to his navel.

"Come here," he said in what she thought had to be the sexiest voice ever heard by anyone, a command she immediately obeyed. Her eyes zeroed in on his full lips with the slightest hint of his fangs pushing out against the lower one and all she could think about was licking them. The instant before she reached her target, he turned and she smiled with her mouth against the base of his jaw, right over his pulse. She teased the skin lightly with her tongue, the scent of him calling forth the hunger she thought had already been more than satisfied. She should have known her appetite would always rise for him. She opened her mouth as he ran his hands down her sides and gripped her hips, pushing them down against his erection, a promise of the reward to come. With that she struck, a load moan vibrating her throat as his blood slid over her tongue and in that moment, she was certain nothing would ever taste as good as Ethan Kellar and he was all hers.

While she drank, Ethan lifted her hips high enough for him to shift his beneath her and position his hard length at her opening. She moaned against his neck and pushed down, sliding her warm folds over his silky steel in one long slow stroke.

"God, Alexa; I love the way your body feels around me," he husked.

She released his neck and whispered against his ear. "I love the way you taste."

Ethan couldn't hold back any longer. In a blur, Alexa was on her back and he pressed between her thighs, moving in long deliberate strokes as he claimed her mouth in a deep kiss. He growled at tasting himself on her lips and her body trembled beneath him. He released her mouth and kissed her shoulder before he scraped his fangs over it and up to the base of her neck. He inhaled her sweet scent before pressing his fangs into the soft skin. The blood slipped down his throat, sending jolts of pleasure through him as her body tightened around him, squeezing his cock relentlessly with the pulses of her climax until he couldn't contain his own any longer. Ethan reared back, growling out into the room with his release, with Alexa's blood coloring his fangs and tongue.

Completely spent, Ethan collapsed beside Alexa.

"I could sleep for a whole day," she said with a satisfied, but sleepy smile.

"Then we should do just that," he replied, lifting up to run his tongue over the twin puncture marks in her neck before he pulled her to his side. Alexa slung her leg over his thighs and her arm over his stomach just before exhaustion claimed her.

CHAPTER 12 - *An Unexpected Ally*

After taking a rather distraught Asana back to her quarters, Chloe finally made her way back to her own room, where she waited anxiously for Lucias to make his next move. Her last vision had given her the first glimmer of hope since her arrival and it had already been ripped away. Her family was safe, but now Lucias knew about Kaleb. She reached for Kaleb's mind and nearly fell over with the pain she felt.

She had to do something. She couldn't just let him suffer like that for hours; it was unbearable.

Before she could think better of it, Chloe opened the door and sped off in search of Lucias.

After traversing several corridors, she found him in the place she knew he would be, but avoided all the same; his playroom, as he liked to call it. For everyone else, apart from Molly, it would be more appropriately named a house of horrors.

She steeled her nerves and scanned inside with her telepathy. Molly was with him, but they'd only just arrived. That made things easier. Going against every instinct in her, Chloe knocked on the door. She immediately sensed Lucias's irritation.

The door flung open. "How dare—"

He stopped cold, speechless for perhaps the first time in his life as he saw Chloe standing there. "Well, this is a pleasant surprise," he said, his voice dripping with feigned sweetness so thick Chloe wished he would choke on it.

"You want to have me in here; I will come willingly if you grant me one favor first," Chloe rushed out, trying to hide the tremble in her voice at what she was about to do.

"Name it," he replied immediately as he felt himself growing harder with the thought. It wasn't that he was even attracted to Chloe; he'd realized that almost immediately upon seeing her sweet and gentle nature, but sex was power and knowing he could never be stronger than this powerful female, he knew he could still dominate her in at least one way with the right leverage. She was a virgin, he was certain of that much and taking that from any woman, human or vampire, strong or weak, gave a man a certain irrevocable power.

"Let Kaleb feed immediately; let him complete the transformation and I will do whatever you ask."

Without another word, Lucias flashed to the phone across the room. "Send the human in to Kaleb. I know what I said, listen to what I'm saying!" he yelled.

"Wait!" Chloe interrupted. "Not the human; it has to be bagged blood. Release the human, wipe their memories and let them go. I don't want him to feed on live blood. That's my condition."

Lucias look at her, puzzled by her request at first, and then he realized her intention and smirked. "It seems you have gotten to know my son rather well," he said, covering the receiver with his hand. "Change of plans, wipe the human female's memories and drop her off in the city," he said, keeping his eyes on Chloe. "Yes, alive, you idiot, and do it tonight. You won't be able to erase enough if we wait another day. Send someone to retrieve ten bags of blood from the cooler and give them to my son immediately."

He hung up the phone and eyed Chloe hungrily. "Satisfied, my dear?"

She swallowed back the bile rising in her throat and forced a smile as she reached for Kaleb's mind; opening a connection to him she knew she would need to get through whatever was to come. His pain burned through it, giving her strength to press on; she only hope it ended quickly, for both of them. "Yes, thank you…Sire," she replied, using the term he forced on everyone else.

"Excellent; now please, join us," he said, gesturing towards the bed where Molly was already laying. Chloe looked at her for the first time since she'd taken her life and turned her into what she had become. Guilt for what she'd done washed over her again, but Molly smiled at her and Chloe couldn't help but notice that something in her had changed beyond her transformation into a vampire.

Chloe stepped inside cautiously, letting the door close behind her. Lucias sped to stand in front of her, his eyes dark with lust. He reached for her shoulder and slowly started to slide her dress down. He'd only moved it a couple of inches when Molly's hand covered his. "Let me do it; you should get comfortable and lie down to watch," she husked in his ear.

Chloe looked at her with confusion, but was grateful to Molly in ways she could never express. Just that small touch of Lucias's hand made her skin crawl.

Taking Molly's suggestion, Lucias finished peeling off his expensive suit and sprawled out on the bed with his hands behind his head. Chloe kept her eyes averted. She'd never seen a naked man in person before, only catching the accidental glimpse in the minds of others. If she could help it, no matter what else happened, she wouldn't let Lucias be the first she saw.

Molly stepped in front of Chloe, blocking Lucias's view as she slid the white dress from her other shoulder and looked into her eyes. Chloe stared back, surprised to find no cruelty, no malicious intent. In fact, if she didn't know better, she'd almost think there was something akin to love in Molly's eyes. She slid Chloe's dress down over her breasts to reveal her white bra and let it drop to the floor, holding Chloe's gaze expectantly. Finally, with a look that seemed a little frustrated, Molly widened her eyes and moved her hand to her temple.

She wanted Chloe to listen to her thoughts.

Chloe was usually far more intuitive, but the strain of being in that room with Lucias had rendered her virtually incapacitated with anxiety. Finally getting Molly's message, she pushed into the petite blonde's mind.

What is it? she asked cautiously.

There's so much I want to say to you. I'm sorry, thank you. I love you, all rattled out of Molly's head in rapid succession, as she urged Chloe to turn and started to work on the clasp of her bra.

I don't know how to describe it, but since I turned, I can feel you all the time. I feel so different; every minute that passes I feel better, good somehow, like I'm becoming a different person. A good person if you can believe that.

Chloe's bra fell to the floor and she turned to face Molly, confused by what she was hearing; so much so that she didn't even think about Lucias watching them.

Then it dawned on her. The infected were bound to Lucias because he fused his blood with the virus, creating something similar to the sire bond he shared with Kaleb, but even more potent. Was it possible that turning Molly with her blood had created a similar bond? It certainly seemed that that was the case.

I'm so sorry for what happened, Molly. I never wanted to hurt you, Chloe sent.

Don't apologize to me, Molly said, reaching to unfasten her own bra. *I attacked you. To be honest, now I can't even understand why, but I owe everything to you. You could have let me die, but instead you saved me and gave me this incredible gift.*

Molly pulled her panties down her legs, slowly bending over. She looked back at Lucias coyly and winked before she stood facing Chloe again.

I know you don't want to do this; I can feel it. I can protect you, just follow my lead and don't say anything, okay? Molly sent, leading Chloe to a chair in the corner.

Chloe nodded almost imperceptibly and followed. Molly pushed her into the chair and moved in close, hovering with her lips almost touching Chloe's. Just trust me; I won't let him near you.

And then Molly pressed her lips to Chloe's ever so gently. Lucias groaned behind them and Molly flashed away pinning him to the bed and sinking her fangs into his chest while Chloe stared into Lucias's eyes, confused and terrified, but she remained silent. Lucias stared at her, holding her gaze until Molly flipped him over to his stomach and started licking down his back effectively diverting his attention. She paused for just a moment and smiled over her shoulder at Chloe. She gave a shaky smile in return and averted her gaze as Molly moved lower.

Uncomfortable and afraid, Chloe stayed in the chair for the next thirty minutes, averting her eyes for most of it, while Molly did as promised, pulling out all the stops so to speak, to keep Lucias so occupied with her that he didn't give Chloe a second thought.

Chloe bolted up on her bed, sensing Lucias's approach. It had been nearly twenty-four hours since she'd slipped out of his playroom, untouched thanks to Molly, while he was in the shower. She thought back to the last silent conversation they'd had and what it meant.

I'm yours, Chloe; I know that as well as my own name. Whatever you ask of me I'll do.

I don't want to control you, Molly; I don't want any of this.

It's yours whether you want it or not. I know some of Lucias's plans. His tongue gets quite loose in bed. I can help you, tell you everything I learn from him, but you should leave before he returns. He'll be ready for more, um, fun by the time he gets out of the shower. I'm not sure I can keep him at bay if he sees you here again.

It wasn't hard to figure out that Lucias would use Chloe to expand his army with turned vampires. Would they all be bound to Chloe like Molly was? Chloe focused, trying to get a clear picture of the future, but it remained elusive, just beyond her grasp.

As if she'd summoned him with her thoughts, Lucias appeared in the doorway.

"It seems I've been neglectful, my dear. My sincere apologies, but Molly can be quite distracting," he said, slipping to sit beside her. "But take heart, we have all the time in the world," he whispered, stroking his fingertips down the side of her face. Chloe fought every natural instinct and smiled up at him. "For now we have more important business to attend to. I hope you've gotten some rest," he said, standing and holding out his hand for her.

Chloe took it reluctantly and followed him.

Chloe's heart jumped before they even entered the room. She could feel him. Kaleb was nearby. Her elation quickly evaporated when they crossed the threshold and she saw him. He was standing across the room, which reminded her of the training room at the compound, except it was larger and devoid of equipment, with eyes locked on some invisible thing, glowing red, absent of any feeling or emotion. He wasn't the first infected she'd seen, of course, but before that moment she'd never really understood what Lucias' infection did. It was almost as if Kaleb wasn't even there anymore and all that remained was an empty shell.

Seeing Kaleb like that, for the first time she truly understood the pain her mother must have felt watching Ethan become infected and then living through the weeks after with the man she loved existing only as a tormented shell of who he once was. It wasn't a fate she would wish on her worst enemy, even though he was right beside her and, in fact, responsible for Kaleb's current state.

"Magnificent, isn't it?" Lucias asked, pulling Chloe from her own thoughts and forcing her to take notice of the hundreds of humans who, based on the erratic combination of so many heartbeats it was like one continuous tone, were unconscious but alive.

Lucias handed her a box containing at least two dozen bags of blood. "You'll need these. It will take a lot of blood to turn all of these humans and there are plenty more where they came from. Not to worry; we're saving some just to feed you for the task."

Chloe's heart ached as she surveyed the room. Where had they all come from? Did they have families, friends who were missing them? Could they ever go back to their lives if she did what was asked? Would Lucias just kill them all anyway if she didn't?

She knew the answer to her last question. Either she turned them or Lucias would kill them and Kaleb and probably all of Asana's family.

She considered requesting that he simply draw her blood and do the job himself, but thought better of it. If he believed she needed to feed her blood to the humans, it would let her keep track of how many he turned and even give her some control over the pace. With Lucias standing over her, Chloe kneeled beside the closest human, a man she guessed to be around twenty. He was handsome, tall, with sandy-blonde hair that reminded her of her uncle. She closed her eyes and called upon the hunger that was always humming just below the surface to get her fangs to drop from her gums. She used them to open the vein at her wrist and pressed the wound to the young man's mouth while she used her other hand to part his lips. Like a baby seeking his mother's teat in the middle of the night, he latched on and suckled instinctually. His sucking became so voracious that Chloe had to yank her wrist free. The moment she did, an infected scooped the man up and carried him off. She wondered to where and thought to push into Lucias's mind to find out, but a little voice told her that she didn't really want to know. She already knew. For every human she turned, Lucias had another who would die to feed them through their transition.

The city of Boston had to be in an uproar with so many going missing in one day.

Chloe looked to Kaleb again, and though his mind was practically blank and he never looked back, she found some small measure of comfort in his presence as she moved from person to person feeding them her blood and watching them be carried off, only stopping to feed when she started to feel weak from the blood loss.

Several hours later, Chloe had made it through about half of the room, when Lucias's words caught her attention. "Molly, I'm leaving you to oversee the process for the next few hours. I have other matters to attend to."

"Of course," Molly said with a bright smile, reaching up and laying a rather vigorous kiss on him.

You know, I thought I actually loved him. Molly said when he left. *Now just looking at him makes me feel sick, but I know I can't let on. Being with me keeps him from you and keeps him happy.*

Chloe looked back at Molly, her eyes full of gratitude. Who would have thought the woman who'd been responsible for her parents' capture, who everyone had thought was so evil, was capable of such self-sacrifice and compassion? Chloe didn't fully understand it all, even with being clairvoyant she hadn't seen that coming, but she was thankful for Molly nonetheless.

CHAPTER 13 - *Family, Friends, and Antiserum*

Cami, so happy to see her brother healthy again, rushed into Ethan's arms, jumping on him like she hadn't done since they were children.

"It's good to see you, too, sis," he said, hugging her tight as everyone poured into the room he shared with Alexa. Though they hadn't slept a whole day, even going to bed only a few hours before dawn they'd managed to sleep through a sunrise and a sunset before waking, both feeling better than they had in weeks.

"You fucking scared me," she whispered as he released her and set her down on her feet.

"Sorry," he replied, giving her a sheepish grin as he extended his hand to Jared. "So here's that man who finally tamed my wild sister's heart!" he exclaimed playfully, shaking Jared's hand, then pulling him close for a manly embrace. "It's good to see you again, Jared."

Jared stepped back, flashing his signature lopsided grin as his eyes cut to Cami with her cheeks glowing red. "I'm working on it," he replied, giving Cami a wink.

"Mamá!" Ethan exclaimed as Josephine walked over and grabbed his face.

"Mi corazón," she said, kissing both of his cheeks before he wrapped his arms around her waist and spun her around.

"It's good to have you back, son," Elijah said, coming up behind Josephine. "You gave us a pretty good scare."

The two men looked at each other, then smiled and hugged hard enough to make it difficult to breathe.

Alexa's parents weren't far behind, hugging them both and chastising Alexa for being so reckless in her quest to save Ethan.

"You know, I *am* the High Commander. Did you ever consider that I might be useful in helping you get to Ethan?" William said, raising his eyebrows at his daughter.

"I was afraid to involve you; if you said no, I'd have to defy you," she said with a smirk, teasing the man who'd been in her life for such a short time, yet felt familiar like a father should be.

"Given what you've learned, and what it means for our people, I think it's safe to say that your defiance, and that of your consorts, whomever they may be," he said cutting his eyes to Cami and Jared with a smirk, "will be forgiven."

"What about Dante?" Alexa asked. She felt Ethan's jealousy flare through their connection, but smiled when she looked at him and saw how hard he was working to conceal it.

"Yes, even The Elite involved will not be punished," William responded.

They all spent the next couple of hours talking over everything that had happened, sharing their joys and their concerns. Chloe was fresh on their minds, but Alexa shared everything she knew from Chloe's visions with Jared and her father, both able to see the images in her mind, while the others listened intently to her descriptions.

"She's so strong; stronger than I ever envisioned," Josephine said to the group. "I have to believe she knew what she was doing when she left."

"That's exactly how I feel," Alexa added, grabbing Josephine's hand. Chloe was young, far too young to be facing the challenges forced upon her, but if anyone could bear it, it was her.

While the others were engrossed in conversation, Jared approached Elijah. "Sir, if I may, I'd like to speak with you, privately."

Cami, always aware of Jared, watched the two men intently. "Of course, Jared. My quarters will afford some privacy," Elijah replied, opening the door. Josephine grinned, a knowing look on her face as she pulled Cami away to distract her.

When they were alone, Jared turned to Elijah, obviously nervous. "Sir, I love your daughter," he blurted out.

"Yes, that much is obvious, but I'm guessing that's not all you have to say," Elijah replied with a laugh as he reached for Jared's shoulder, trying to calm his nerves.

"Yes, you see, I, well, I want to ask Cami to be my mate, to marry me," he finally stuttered out.

Elijah crossed one arm over his chest and stroked his chin with the other as if he was deep in thought, obviously teasing, but the joke was lost on Jared in all his anxiety.

"Well, son, my daughter is a strong woman; she's over two-hundred years old and definitely knows her own mind by now. Of course, I certainly can't answer for her, but I appreciate you recognizing that her family, her mother, brother, and I are from another time, one where it was the custom to ask a father's permission before proposing marriage. Though I think you might have missed the memo about some of the other conditions regarding courting a woman and marriage," Elijah joked again.

Jared, who was usually pretty cocky and confident, felt the color rush from his face when he understood Elijah's meaning.

Elijah burst into a fit of laughter. "Lighten up, Jared! I'm not so old

174

fashioned," he said, struggling to be serious again. Regaining his composure, he continued. "Jared, you've managed to do something no man has accomplished in centuries. My daughter has let you into her heart. That is no small feat. If she thinks you're good enough, I won't argue it and, as it stands, with what I've known of you in this short time, I couldn't wish for a better mate for my little girl. But I have to warn you, she's never been overly receptive to traditional ideas of family and marriage. What will you do if she says no?" Elijah asked.

"Sir, when I first fell for Cami she fought it and I told her that I would wait for her for as long as it took. If she refuses my proposal, I'll ask her every day for the rest of our lives. She's the one. It doesn't matter how long it takes her to realize it; I already know."

Every hint of joking faded from Elijah's face and he yanked Jared into his arms. "She's lucky to have you and I would be proud to call you my son, Jared," he said, squeezing him hard before releasing him and speeding to the table where sat an excellent bottle of scotch. He poured two fingers in a tulip-shaped glass then inclined the bottle to Jared in a silent question. Jared nodded and Elijah splashed the brown liquid into the second glass before picking them both up and passing one to Jared.

"A toast; to strong women! My family is full of them and I wish the same joy for your family," he said to Jared with a wink as they clinked their glasses together. "To strong women," Jared repeated, and downed his drink in one gulp.

"Now comes the hard part," Elijah said, clamping Jared's soldier.

"You have to ask her."

✧

"I've continued to watch for her since the day she was born, but with the blocking charm or without, Chloe's future has always eluded me," Josephine replied to Ethan and Alexa's questioning, "but there was one vision; it wasn't specifically focused on Chloe, even so, I saw her there, I'm sure of it. And Lucias was there as well. It won't be of much help and I've already shared it with the Commander, but I saw two armies gathered, Lucias's and The Elite, not far from the compound."

"Gracias, Mamá. Thank you," Elijah said, giving her a quick hug. "Just let us know if you see anything more."

"Of course, mi corazón," Josephine replied as Elijah and Jared reentered the room.

"What have you two been up to?" Cami asked, sidling up to Jared.

"Just a little male bonding," Elijah responded with wink.

Before Cami could press either of them further, the buzzer at the door sounded. Being closest, Jared hit the button to respond. "Yes?"

"It's Commander Claesson. I need to speak with Alexa."

Alexa looked at Ethan, andthen flashed to the door. "Yes, Commander?" she queried when it opened.

"We need you back in the lab."

"Already? Can't it wait? We want to spend some time with our families." Ethan questioned, his tone bordering on annoyance. Alexa had spent hours there the day before while he had to watch pint after pint of her blood being siphoned from her arm.

"I'm afraid it can't. Reports are coming in from the city and it's not good," he said, giving William a pointed look. "Lucias is making a move; I can't say for certain what he's up to, but we need to be prepared for the worst. That means we need as much antiserum as you can stand to make."

"Ethan, we have to do what we can to help, for Chloe," Alexa whispered to him. He couldn't argue, so he simply sighed and nodded to the Commander.

Within a few seconds, the couple found themselves back in the room where they were first reunited. Alexa glanced quickly at the cell where Dante remained with Layla. He was sitting with his back to her, partially dressed in what was left of his tattered clothes, and he was covered in fresh blood. Alexa looked to the Commander. "What's going on; why are they still in there?" she asked.

"Layla is still infected," the Commander replied, "we have to maintain an abundant source of the virus; for now, she's it."

"You can't do that to them!" she yelled, looking to Dante who was pacing at the front of the cell, obviously pissed.

"Calm down, Alexa. Right now we don't have a choice. The virus cycles through your system too quickly and we don't have the time to figure out how to replicate the process, nor are we even certain we can replicate it," Dr. Jones interjected.

"I'm guessing Dante didn't take that news very well," Alexa said, looking at her friend with compassion and concern, only to see him staring at Ethan with murderous intent; realizing he might be angry about more than Layla's continued infection. "Is it safe for him to be in there with her?" she asked, earning a hard glare from Ethan. Clearly, the feeling between the two men was mutual.

"Easy, tiger. He's a friend, remember? I just don't want him to get hurt," she added, stroking Ethan's well-muscled chest, which seemed to calm him down just a little. He'd managed to hide his jealously in front of their families, but with Dante in the same room, basically provoking him, there wasn't a chance in hell that he could hold it back.

"Safe or not, he wouldn't come out even if we could find a way to get him out without risking Layla escaping, but something good has come of that" Claesson replied. "As you can see, Layla has fed from Dante since he was cured, yet he shows no signs of infection; proof that the effects of the antiserum are permanent. That's excellent news for us. Once we cure one of Lucias's men, he can't reinfect them and we'll be able to vaccinate our civilian population, rendering what has been Lucias's greatest weapon all but completely useless."

She looked up at Ethan. He shrugged his shoulders. It wasn't really a choice, but something else weighed heavily on his mind.

'I'm not so sure the virus is his greatest weapon anymore," Ethan added. "He has Chloe now; we don't know what she's capable of, or how he might use her in his fight for power."

"Of course, I'll do whatever I can to help, but Ethan is right; what about Chloe? Are we any closer to finding where he's keeping her?"

"We're working on it. Ethan's information really helped, but this antiserum will give us the advantage we need to move on that intel a lot sooner than we'd originally anticipated."

"I still think if you let me go out with the next team, I will be able to help more. Seeing the areas might trigger some other memories of the location where he held us."

"I appreciate that, Ethan; we might take you up on that at some point, just not yet."

"And what about my other request?" Ethan pressed.

"You know I'm all for it, but it's not just *my* call. I'll keep working on it, but I can't make any promises," Claesson replied, inching towards the door; eager to move on to other business now that he had delivered Alexa to Dr. Jones.

"What other request?" Alexa asked, looking to Ethan, then the Commander. She hadn't heard Ethan ask for anything and she'd been by his side practically every moment. Claesson took that as his cue to disappear.

Ethan figured it was as good a time as any to tell her. "When the time comes, I want to fight, but your father is against it because of you and my history with Lucias."

"No, no way!" Alexa said, shaking her head. "Thank God for my father. I've lost you to that monster once, and he has my daughter. I'm not going to let you walk right back to him to satisfy some macho need for vengeance. Let the soldiers fight so that when we finally get Chloe back, it won't be at the cost of her father's life. You can't do that to her. You can't do that to me."

"Amor—" Ethan started, but stopped. She was right; he was driven by a need for vengeance and there was nothing he could say to make her understand. "You're right; I'm sorry, it was a foolish request."

Alexa stared at him, searching through their bond to be certain that he meant it. Ethan gave her a sexy grin and slid his arms around her waist, lowering his mouth to hers in a passionate kiss that stole her breath.

Dr. Jones cleared his throat. "We really should get started," he said without looking at the couple still in each other's arms.

When Ethan released her, Alexa looked up at him through her lashes, with lust burning in her eyes. "Just because you can kiss me senseless doesn't mean I'm going to forget about this," she said as she moved towards the doctor. She knew Ethan far too well to believe he would give up so easily, but she didn't want to fight, and instead resolved to keep a close eye on him. If he wanted to fight Lucias, she probably couldn't stop him, but he would think twice if she insisted on going with him.

✧

"There's no way I'm leaving, Amor. If he's just a friend, why does he keep eyeing me like he's jealous, like he wants to rip out my throat every time I get close to you," Ethan asked, storming around the containment unit while Doctor Jones was getting set up.

Alexa looked toward Dante again. There was no denying that he was not a fan of her mate, but she suspected that the reason had nothing to do with her.

"Trust me, my love; it doesn't have anything to do with me," she said, taking Ethan's hand and holding his gaze while she kissed his palm. "Dante is a mirror."

"What does that have to do with it, Alexa? You kissed him and it clearly meant more to him than it did to you. Look at him!" Ethan yelled, pulling his hand away and pointing at Dante, who was indeed staring at Ethan with eyes full of hatred.

"I think he saw; I think he knows," Alexa whispered. Ethan looked at her and raised his hands in question. "About you and Layla," she continued in answer, feeling her stomach flop at the mention of it. "He's absorbed my telepathy before. I think it gets easier every time and, when I bit him, I had just been thinking about it; you were probably thinking about it. Maybe she was, too. He could have seen it from any of us."

Ethan looked at Dante again, then at Layla sprawled out on the floor behind him and, though they couldn't hear him, Dante let out a growl when his eyes were on Layla.

"Well, shit," Ethan said, turning away.

"I'll explain it to him; he'll understand," Alexa stated, realizing that no amount of explanation would make Dante feel any better about Ethan and Layla fucking. Ethan seemed to know it as well, based on the cynical look he gave in response to her statement. "Okay, maybe he won't understand, but I'll help him deal with it. I'm not going to be able to do that with you here hovering behind me, growling at every turn as a constant reminder. It's bad enough I have to deal with her listening to everything we say; even if she might not care now because she's infected. Once they've collected enough antiserum, she'll be cured and we'll all have to figure out a way to deal with what happened and move on. This is the first step. So please trust me and just give me five minutes to speak with him," Alexa pleaded, placing a hand on Ethan's cheek.

"Five minutes; not a millisecond longer," Ethan agreed reluctantly. Alexa stood up on her toes and kissed his cheek. "I love you, Ethan," she whispered before she spun him around and started ushering him to the door.

"I truly do not like this," Ethan said over his shoulder.

"But you love me, and you're doing this for me," she replied, giving him a little wave before the door closed between them.

"I don't understand how you're so calm about this," Dante gritted out through the intercom at the front of the cell he shared with Layla.

Luckily, she was asleep in the corner, still blood-drunk from her last feeding. In order to draw enough samples to produce the antiserum, Dr. Jones was granted most of the remaining blood stores on the compound to feed Layla. It had taken a while, but thanks to the collection system the doctor was able to rig up and the preternatural healing of the vampire body, after this round of extraction they would have more than enough blood from Layla to generate sufficient antiserum to cure the whole of Lucias's army and then some. While the ultimate goal was to continue production until the whole vampire population was vaccinated, the research team was confident that they would be able to synthesize the virus long before they ran out of samples from Layla. Unfortunately for Alexa, they still weren't able to pinpoint what it was in her blood that allowed her body to generate the antiserum, so she would remain integral to the process for the foreseeable future.

"Because it was beyond either of their control, and you know it. Besides, if we're being honest, you and Layla weren't even a couple at the time. If I recall, there was something about a human in that bar the night she went missing bouncing around in that head of yours, too, so don't be such a hypocrite."

Dante's eyes shot to Alexa for a moment, his expression shocked, then ashamed. She was right; he'd had no claim on Layla at the time. Ethan was her bonded mate and she'd somehow found a way to deal with the situation; at least that's what she claimed. She might feel differently when Layla was cured.

"I know it's hard, Dante, but I'm just asking you to try. In a few minutes, Layla's going to be cured and you'll both be out of here. Try to focus on that; the second chance you're about to get to make things right with her. You're important to me; I want for us to remain friends. I want all of us to be friends, but that is going to be impossible if you're growling at my mate and giving him the evil eye every time you see each other. It's hard for him, too, knowing there was something between us, even if it only turned out to be friendship; all he can think about is that we kissed."

"Okay, I'll try, but I can't make any promises."

"And what about Layla? What are you going to tell her about everything? Will you tell her that you know?"

"Yeah, I have to. Like you said, this is my second chance to make things right. I can't start out keeping secrets." The shame she'd seen in his eyes before returned. "She's had to deal with me and other women before," he whispered, "I just hope she can do it again, because I swear it's the last time. She's all I want now."

Alexa smiled at him, her eyes full of understanding. "She's a lucky woman." Alexa turned to the door then stopped. "So we're clear, there will be no growling, chest puffing, or muttered threats directed at my husband when you're out of there, right?" she asked a teasing edge to her voice, though it was a legitimate concern.

"I said I'd try. I'll give you the growling and chest puffing, but you have to let me keep the muttered threats," he joked back.

"I guess I'll take that," Alexa said with a triumphant smile.

"Seriously, though, thank you, Alexa, for everything. I don't know what I would have done without you. You saved me; you saved all of us," Dante said, pressing his palm to the glass the same way Alexa had done when she first came back. Alexa's eyes welled up with tears as she placed her hand over his and nodded; too choked up to say anything else before she released the button and sped to the door.

Alexa smiled up at Ethan from her semi-supine position. Dr. Jones had managed to get a recliner dragged into the lab for her to relax in while her body did its magic.

"I'm proud of you," she said, rubbing her thumb over the back of his hand that was linked with hers. "You didn't even look at Dante when you came in. That's progress," she teased.

"Amor, I will always do whatever I can to please you," his words were sweet, but the look in his eyes gave them a more delicious meaning. Alexa groaned. "Ethan, you're such a tease," she whispered.

He responded with a soft, slow kiss.

Dr. Jones cleared his throat behind him. It seemed he had to do that a lot when he was around Ethan and Alexa. "We're ready to begin."

Ethan vacated his seat in order to get out of the way, while the doctor set up the machine that would continuously draw Alexa's blood. He placed a cooler filled with bags of Layla's blood on the other side of her chair. "That should do it for now; just sit back and relax. I'll be here the whole time, so just let me know if either of you need anything."

"What about Layla?" Alexa asked as her blood made its way along the clear tubing and emptied into the first of many collection bags.

"I administered the antiserum a few minutes ago and expect she'll be free of the virus at any moment. She and Dante will remain contained for a little while until we confirm with a blood test, but I expect they'll be out of here in the next thirty-minutes or so."

"Thank you," Alexa said gratefully as she glanced across the room to Layla's cell. She focused her telepathy and beamed at Ethan while he took the seat beside her again. It warmed her heart to feel Dante's relief and happiness.

Ethan looked at her curiously, feeling the sudden lift in her mood. "They're so happy in there. I wish you could feel it; then you'd know you have nothing to worry about with Dante."

"I can feel it, Amor. I feel it in you, here," he said, placing his palm over her heart and pulling hers to his. "If Dante's happiness brings you such joy, I wish him as much as anyone in the world."

As promised, it wasn't long before Dr. Jones opened the door to release Dante and Layla. The pair stepped out, arm in arm, looking as content as anyone could covered in dried blood and wearing drab hospital gowns that the doctor had provided for them, after confirming Layla was cured, to replace the blood-soaked and practically disintegrated rags they'd had in the cell.

Alexa guessed a shower and some quality alone time for the couple was in order. She wanted to call out to Dante, but thought better of it. Ethan was trying and Dante said he would as well, but their wounds were fresh and she didn't want to push her luck. It was impossible for her to hide her shock when Ethan sped across the room and put his hand out to Dante. It didn't help her state when Dante looked to her, smiled, and shook Ethan's hand before they headed her way with Layla in tow. Perhaps she had underestimated them both.

"Alexa, this is Layla," Dante said, presenting the woman he loved, who was a complete mess at the time, as if she was the most precious thing in the world.

Layla flashed to Alexa and hugged her tightly, lifting her up slightly from her chair before Alexa could even think to react. "Thank you," she said, continuing to hold Alexa for a moment. It seemed that everyone was full of surprises.

"Oh, um, you're welcome. It's nice to finally meet you," Alexa replied when she'd finally composed herself. Suddenly all of the animosity she'd felt toward Layla melted away, seeming like something from a bad and very distant nightmare.

"I don't mean to be rude, but Layla and I are a few decades overdue for some time alone," Dante said, taking Layla's hand, already moving towards the door. Layla giggled, sounding more like a school girl than a centuries-old vampire soldier who'd virtually been brought back from the dead only minutes before.

The matching hospital gowns were discarded before the door to Dante's room had fully closed. He scooped Layla up and cradled her in his arms as he made his way to the bathroom. Setting her down, he flashed around the room, turning on the bath and shower and gathering supplies, returning to her side only seconds later.

Dante cupped Layla's face in his hands and pressed a soft, reverent kiss on her lips. "I'm going to take care of you, okay?" She simply nodded her response. He led her to the shower where they both stepped inside, just long enough to let the water wash away the bulk of the blood still covering most of their bodies. He turned the water off and picked her up again. A moment later, she was settled comfortably in the tub between Dante's powerful thighs, her back to him as he began to wash her body. Neither of them spoke, instead letting their actions do the talking for them. Layla circled her finger over Dante's knee while he gently scrubbed her scalp. They continued in that fashion for a long time, with Dante gently washing and caring for Layla until he was satisfied that every trace of the past weeks had been washed away. He washed his own body in a rush, before lifting Layla from the tub and wrapping her in a towel.

Her naked body was perhaps the most beautiful Dante had ever seen and, while it was impossible to hide his desire with every part of him exposed, he didn't want to make it about sex. Sex he'd had, lots of it with lots of women, and it never meant anything. Layla meant everything and he was going to do whatever it took to prove that to her.

Layla turned to face him and kissed his well-defined pec as she slid her hands down the front of his body, letting her hands travel over the chiseled planes of his abs. She reached for his length, but he grabbed her hand before she could touch him. She looked up at him, confused, but intrigued.

"Not here, not yet," he whispered, bending down to kiss her gently. "Come on," he said taking her hand, "we should get dressed."

"Really?" she asked, obviously surprised. She'd known Dante a long time; this was definitely a side of him she'd never seen.

"Yes, I want to talk."

"Okay," she said reluctantly and followed him to the bedroom. A minute later, thanks to their supernatural speed and Dante's forethought to ask Jasmine to move some of Layla's clothes to his room, they were dressed.

"So now that you have me here, just where you want me, fully dressed," Layla teased as she rifled through her bag, "what did you want to talk about?" she asked, standing to run a brush through her hair. When Dante didn't respond, she turned to find him on one knee in front of her, wearing an uncertain smile. She gasped when her eyes went to the little black box in his trembling hand.

"No," she said in disbelief, "wait, not no to you!" she added, seeing the hurt and disappoint flash in his eyes, "It's just I, I can't, is this real?" she stuttered, her eyes filling up with tears.

"Layla Jones, I'm an idiot," he began, earning a laugh. "You've been right here in front of me, one of my closest friends, yet somehow I didn't see you, not the way I should have. You've been there for me in ways no one else has, and though I know I don't deserve it, that I don't deserve you, I'm hoping you'll give me the chance to be there for you every day for the rest of our long lives. It took losing you for me to finally realize that you are the only one for me. I love you, Layla. Can you find it somewhere in that amazing heart of yours to forgive me and grant me the unfathomable honor of becoming my bonded mate and wife?

Her answer was a hug so fast and hard that they fell to the ground and then into a joyful fit of laughter.

CHAPTER 14 - *Chaos in Boston*

"Sir, reports have been coming in from our sources in the city faster than I can keep up, not to mention what's all over the news. It's utter chaos out there. At least two-hundred humans have been grabbed so far tonight. After what happened last week, people are panicking," Jester said, flying around the IT room, pulling up files on various screens.

"And we're certain it's Lucias?" William asked, looking to Commander Claesson as he ran his hand down the side of his face in frustration.

"There's no doubt," he replied, pointing to a video that Jester had just put up on the main screen. "Jester yanked this off a site twenty minutes ago."

"Fuck me," the High Commander said as he watched the clip. Two large men flew into view, moving far faster than the average human. One of them, with a single hand, yanked the driver's side door completely off a dark compact car before scooping up the two-hundred-plus-pound driver as if he weighed no more than a bag of groceries. Meanwhile, his counterpart grabbed two other men who had yet to enter the vehicle, tucked them under his arms and turned in the direction of the camera, revealing his glowing red eyes before they all disappeared in a blur.

"Based on the police report, this was shot by the driver's girlfriend who was still in the apartment at the time. She turned over the phone used to shoot this to the police when she filed the report and, from what I can tell, she didn't share it with anyone before then. Turns out one of the officers at the station uploaded it to the Internet. We got lucky; the phone was still on so I was able to corrupt the original video and the one the officer sent to himself to get it online."

"Thank God; the last thing we need is for something like this to be our kind's introduction to the world," William stated as he sank into a chair.

"It could be worse; so far the infected don't appear to be feeding on any of the humans, at least not in public," Jester added, "but with all of the attacks last week, people are going to realize there's a connection and start asking questions.

"My guess is that Lucias is keeping these humans alive, collecting blood slaves to power up his army in preparation for battle," Claesson said, though in the back of his mind he knew there was something else to it. Lucias already had plenty of blood slaves and no doubt some steady connections with a variety of blood dealers; he could see grabbing a few more, but hundreds? Something didn't quite add up.

"So it appears we have run out of time."

"I'm afraid it looks that way, my lord. Thank God for Alexa; she's down in the lab as we speak, helping get the rest of the antiserum we'll need."

"What about the other preparations?" William asked.

"I'll speak to Martinez as soon as we're done here. We'll have the rations within the hour and, if I'm correct, Lucias will be right where we want him when the sun goes down tomorrow; especially if we go ahead with the broadcast tonight," Claesson replied calmly.

"Make the call, Jester. Set the meeting for midnight. We can have our people on the air by 10 pm on the west coast if the other leaders agree."

"Whatever the fuck happened before, I don't care. As far as I'm concerned, you were operating under extreme coercion, Dante was mentally unstable, temporary insanity or some shit, and Alexa isn't under my jurisdiction. Her father has already made it clear that, in light of recent events and Alexa's contributions to our cause, he wants everyone involved in helping her pardoned from any further repercussions, so who am I to argue?" Commander Claesson said, pacing the floor of his office. "Dante and Layla will be out of containment soon, if they're not already, but neither of them will be fit for duty tonight and I need someone local I can trust implicitly. That's why I want you to take point on a mission to the city."

"Of course, sir, whatever you need," Martinez said gratefully, glad to hear that his friends were going to be okay and that none of them would be brought up on any formal charges for their actions.

"Good man," he said, moving to the maps on his desk. "First, our civilian scouts report that Lucias's men have been setting up here, here and here every night after sunset," he said, indicating three circles on the large piece of paper located fairly close to the walls of the compound. "I don't think we can move anyone or anything through the front or back entrances without getting ambushed, so the secret tunnel that leads to the center of the city is our only option. The space is tight, so we'll need to keep the team small, just enough men to pull the carts once they're weighed down; six guys should do it."

"Why can't we just wait until the morning; let the sun take care of Lucias's men for us and use whatever entrance we want?"

"It has to be tonight; we can't afford to wait. The shit has been hitting the fan out there since sunset. I don't know what Lucias is up to, but hundreds of humans have gone missing in the last couple of hours and there have been witness reports claiming anything from big men high on PCP to the devil himself being responsible."

"Shit; they're leaving witnesses again?" Martinez said, shaking his head in disbelief.

"Yeah, and it won't be long before the v-word comes into play with infected running around the city unopposed. There was even a video of one of the abductions. Jester managed to take care of it before it went viral, but who knows how long before something else pops us? By some miracle there haven't been any witness accounts of public feeding this time around, at least so far. It seems the attacks last week were purely a distraction; this is something different, but one of them could still lose control at any time."

"What do you need me to do, sir?" Martinez asked, studying the plans.

"I need you to take a team of five men and meet with Davies, here," he said, indicating a spot about two blocks from Blood Runners, the vampire bar where Layla was kidnapped.

"Davies, the blood dealer?" Martinez questioned, more than a little surprised given what he knew about the Commander and the rumors he'd heard about Davies.

"Yes; if it goes against your moral sensibilities, get the fuck over it!" Claesson yelled, more angry with himself than with Martinez's question. In addition to the stress of the chaos erupting in the city and his lack of sleep due to the intricate planning he'd been involved in all week, being forced to work with his degenerate brother-in-law rubbed him wrong in more ways than he could name. Not to mention, due to the severe shortage of blood, he'd gone without feeding longer than he should. "We don't have a choice; keeping Dante and Layla from draining each other dry ate up most of our stores and Dr. Jones used most of what was left on Layla and Alexa to make the antiserum. We need to be ready to fight at a moment's notice and, with all of the soldiers in from other compounds to feed, we need more blood now. I need everyone strong and well-fed if we're going to stand a chance against an entire army of infected. We might have a cure, but that won't save us from the fight."

"I'm sorry, sir. I don't have a problem; I'll work with whomever you tell me to."

"Good. That brings me to the second part of the mission. As I'm sure you know, that little fucker happens to be my wife's brother and, for some reason I'll never understand, she trusts him. With the way things are going out there, I'll feel a lot better if they were on the compound, so in addition to the blood, he's bringing her and my daughter to the rendezvous point. Choose your team and be outside the pit in thirty minutes. Jester will set you up with comm equipment and Jackson will be waiting with some new bullets in case you run into any infected, which is a strong possibility. The boys in the lab haven't had much time, so you're only going to have a handful of bullets with antiserum. The policy is to use those if you can get close enough. If not, use the silver bullets to disable, silver nitrate or head shots only if absolutely necessary; but so we're clear, if my wife and daughter are in danger, choose the latter."

"Understood, sir; thank you" Martinez said before disappearing through the door. Commander Claesson sank down in his seat and took a couple of deep breaths, trying to steady himself before he got back to work dealing with the shit storm Lucias was stirring up all over Boston. He hated that he couldn't be the one to retrieve his family, but he had a greater responsibility to their kind as they moved through the challenges ahead.

Martinez stepped into the training room in search of the three men he wanted for the impending operation. He took two strides into the room when Captain Erikson stopped him.

"Hey, Martinez, I heard there might be a small team heading out on a supply run tonight or tomorrow. That true?"

"Where'd you hear that?"

Erikson motioned for them to step into another room. "I am still the head of the High Commander's security team. That might not mean much to all of you here on the compound, but it means something to the High Commander and the Agency. I've been kept in the loop on the general comings and goings on the compound. It's necessary for me to ensure Mr. Ryan's safety."

"Look, man, I'm sorry; I don't have any beef with you. Whatever the issue is with you and Claesson, it has nothing to do with me. I just follow orders," Martinez said, raising his hands in mock surrender. "You heard right, we're heading out tonight; just a small team to stock up on blood and escort a couple civilians into the compound."

"Any chance I could tag along?"

"You should probably clear that with the Commander first."

"Listen, like you said, there's some bad blood between me and Claesson, but I honestly don't know why. He's pretty much been hassling me and my men since we got here. I just need to get outside the walls for a few minutes; make a couple phone calls to my family and reach out to people for a couple of my men. We came here in such a rush there was no time for personal communication and we've been on physical and digital lockdown ever since; no one knows anything about where we are and you can imagine how worried our families are. Some of my guys have mates, kids. Help me out here, just to put their minds at ease. I won't get in the way," Captain Erikson said, pleading his case. "Just imagine if it was you. You're lucky enough to have your mate here. Think how hard it would be with her on the outside having no way to reach you and no idea where you were or what was going on."

"Bro, I'd like to help you, but I'm already on thin ice with the whole mess down in the containment unit. I've got to ask the Commander first."

"Mess in containment?" Erikson asked, raising his eyebrows though he'd already heard more than whispers about what had occurred. It was part of the reason he was so desperate to get out of the compound.

"I'm not getting into that; if the High Commander wants to fill you in, that's his business."

"Fine, I get that; but about my leaving, you know what Claesson's going to say. Listen, how about this? You don't actually take me with you, just let me know when you're going and you bring up the rear of the team. Ignore me and I'll find my way out behind you and keep my distance. That way you have plausible deniability if anything goes down."

"But how will you get back in without anyone seeing you? Only Elite can access the entrance from either side. If you're not back here when we pass through, you'll be stuck outside."

"Just let me worry about that. I'll make it back in time."

Martinez sighed. "Fine, but to be clear, I don't know shit about it if anyone asks," he said, heading back to the training room.

"Understood," Erikson replied to his back.

"Is it safe to assume that Martinez has filled you in on the nature of your mission tonight?" Commander Claesson said, looking around at the other five men in the corridor. Satisfied with their affirmative nods, he continued. "We need this blood and we need it tonight. Many on the compound have gone without, due to some unavoidable shortages, including me, and, as I'm sure you can tell, things are starting to happen pretty fast," he continued, cutting his eyes to the commotion in the pit where Jester was rushing around setting up equipment while the High Commander paced, looking over notes. "But as you can all guess, I need for this to go off without a hitch for far more personal reasons."

Commander Claesson tapped on the glass and waved Jester over. An instant later, the curly-haired vampire appeared in the doorway with his arms full of radios and earpieces.

"Jester has modified these radios so they'll work despite the communications blackout. I'll keep the channel open on my end until you're back here safe and sound. As a precaution, I've assembled a backup team that will be on standby at the entrance to the tunnel. You catch a whiff of anything, you call it in, Martinez; you got me?"

"Yes, sir."

"The city is crawling with infected, so move quickly and quietly. I know most of you are probably ready to get your hands on some of those bastards, but you are not to engage them if you can avoid it. You'll get your chance for that soon enough. I just confirmed with Davies that he'll be at the rendezvous point on time. There will be two carrier vans; the one parked closest to the street is the priority. Davies will have his own team guarding the shipment on his end and they're going to stay with you until you're back through the tunnel to make sure no one tries to follow you. I don't really trust him, but he loves his sister; he won't risk putting her in danger. Martinez, you stay until that door is closed, no exception," the Commander said, pinning Martinez with his stare to emphasize the importance.

"One more thing I want you all to keep in mind; some of you might not need the reminder, but Lucias's men, the infected, some of them used to be our friends, our neighbors, family even. It might be hard to see it in them now, but most of them are victims, civilians snatched from their homes by our true enemy. There aren't many among us who haven't lost someone to that bastard's dirty virus. For the first time, we have a chance to get some of those people back, so if it comes to a fight, while you are not to compromise the mission or yourselves, the directive from the Agency in all engagement with the infected is to disable if possible and kill only if absolutely necessary. Understood?"

"Yes, sir," they said in unison.

"All right. Head down to the armory; Jackson's got some new toys for you," the Commander said, feeling amped up. He wasn't sure if it was due to the coming battle that was so close he could taste it, the fact he was going to be seeing his family within the hour, or that after thousands of years living in secrecy, his people were stepping out into the open for the whole world to see.

"Commander, if I may, what's going on in there?" Martinez asked, looking through the glass wall into the pit as the rest of his team left for the armory.

"Just the end of the world as we know it," he replied.

A confused expression covered Martinez's face. "Don't worry; the High Commander is about to make an announcement that will explain everything. You'll hear what's going on before you leave."

Martinez nodded slowly as he watched the leader of the vampire race pacing anxiously. It was definitely something big.

"One more thing, sir. Captain Erikson approached me earlier wanting to stowaway on this mission." The Commander's gaze snapped to his face. "I'm sorry, sir, he was rather convincing in pleading the case to get out to contact family for his men, so I agreed to look the other way, but in light of all this, I'm having second thoughts. I just thought I should let you know and assure you that I'll make sure he doesn't sneak through."

"No, Martinez. Don't say a word; just let him through."

"But, sir, what if he doesn't get back in time? If you want to let him tag along, shouldn't we bring him through with the team? As it is, he'll only have about thirty minutes on the outside before we seal the door."

"Like I said, don't say anything. The communications blackout is going to be lifted tonight and Erikson will know that before you leave. I think he's up to something, and if he still wants to go after the High Commander's announcement, I'll know I'm right."

"So do you want me to wait for him before I seal the door?"

"No, once my family is inside and the blood is loaded, you shut it. If he really goes, he doesn't plan on coming back."

CHAPTER 15 - *Blood and Bullets*

Commander Claesson entered the pit and looked toward the High Commander, who was still lost in his notes. He wondered if he should tell him what he'd just learned about Erikson. After all, he was the head of William's personal guard.

"My lord, whenever you're ready to begin just press this button and you'll be heard in every room on the grounds, even the outbuildings," Jester said, sliding the piece of equipment over to Williams's seat.

Claesson opened his mouth to speak, but then snapped it shut. If he said anything to William about the Captain, he would likely want to confront Erikson. The Commander didn't know what it was about him, but he'd had a bad feeling about Captain Erikson from the start and he needed to get to the bottom of it. William was far too close to the man who'd protected him for centuries to see that something wasn't right. Before he could second guess his decision to keep the information to himself, the High Commander cleared his throat and began.

"Good evening. As you are all no doubt aware, the last few weeks have been a particularly trying time for our people. Living within the protective walls of the compound over this time, we have requested a great deal from all of you; cutting off communication with the outside world; separating many of you from your friends and family. I assure you, we have done this with only the best interests of our people, both here and outside, at heart. Until now, many of you have been left in the dark to protect those interests, but tonight I am here to tell you that we are all stepping into the light."

"For centuries we've fought not only for the safety of our people, but also for that of the humans among whom we have lived and worked. Now we will ask that they join us in that fight. In the next couple of hours, leaders around the world, both human and vampire, will be making an announcement that will change the world. That our kind, vampires, do in fact exist, and that we have shared this earth for thousands of years, unable to reveal ourselves for fear of persecution, but that now, when the freedom of the world we all love is at stake, we are willing to take that risk that the faith our shared desire for freedom will unite our people."

"Lucias Thorne seeks to rob us of that freedom, to make slaves of us all, vampire and human alike, using biological warfare to control our minds and bodies. He has abducted at least two-hundred humans tonight for use as blood slaves and God knows what else. Let me be the first to tell you, his efforts have been in vain. After searching for more years than I care to count, we have indeed found a cure for Lucias's virus. I know that some of you have lost love ones to this unforgiving disease, but no more. As we speak, the antiserum is being manufactured in the old Adam's shoe factory outside of the city, where our human allies have worked tirelessly over the last day to set up a secure and efficient laboratory. By the end of the week, we will have enough of the cure to save every infected vampire alive today and within a few months, enough to vaccinate every healthy vampire against infection. I share this to highlight the partnership our people already have in place with Boston's founding human families. That partnership will no doubt aid us in demonstrating to the humans that we are not their enemy and they should not fear us."

"I know many of you are afraid, I must admit that I am as well, but the time has come for us to stand up. Our leaders have worked for many years on this plan of integration and we have prepared for a variety of contingencies to protect our people. There are a select group of powerful humans, like the Boston families who gave us this compound and the new lab, who have known of our kind for generations, who have kept our secret, and who have agreed to give their public support to our people throughout this trying time and into the future."

"In light of this development, Commander Claesson will lift the communications blackout immediately following the first broadcast so that you will be free to talk to your friends and families on the outside. I know that you all have a lot of questions right now, but I trust many of those will be addressed in the broadcast. The physical lockdown will remain effective until further notice, but you should all know that we don't expect that to last long. Revealing the existence of our people and warning humans about the infected takes away some of Lucias's power and he will be reluctant to send his men out into the city once they are exposed."

"I want to thank all of you for your tireless efforts; I know every soldier here has gone above and beyond their already-taxing duties to help us prepare for the battle at hand and I ask you all to take the remainder of the evening off to rest, watch the announcement, and spend some well-deserved time catching up with your friends and families."

"Can you believe all this?" Jackson said as he loaded antiserum rounds into clips for Martinez and his team.

"Not really. I guess we always knew it would happen eventually; just always seemed like it was a lot farther off," Martinez replied, sliding one of his guns into its holster.

"The world is going to get really crazy for a while."

"It's already crazy in Boston; Lucias has left us with no choice. If The Agency didn't bring us out in the open, his men would, and not in a way that would make humans feel particularly accepting. At least this way, they have another enemy to focus on, even if they do hate what we are," Martinez added, stopping as Rachel walked into the room. What was it going to be like for their child, growing up in a world where humans knew about vampires?

"I just wanted to wish you luck," she said, giving him a kiss on the cheek, "and let you know that we'll be waiting for you in our room to watch the big news when you get back."

"It's just an easy supply run." Martinez dropped to his knees and kissed her belly. "I love you, both of you," he said, looking up at Rachel.

"We love you, too, John," she replied. "So, why don't you join me when you're done setting them up here, Uncle Jackson?" Rachel offered, reaching up to rub her brother's hair.

"Bro, why does being born one minute sooner, over a hundred years ago make your wife think she can treat me like a kid?" Jackson asked teasingly of his twin sister's husband.

"You should be used to it by now," Martinez joked, getting back to his feet. He smacked Rachel's bottom as she walked away, laughing.

Martinez tossed clips loaded with antiserum rounds to the five men he'd selected for the mission and added two to his own weapons harness. "Keep an eye on your sister for me," he said, pulling Jackson into a manly embrace, "and if we get held up, I stashed my blood rations in the back of the fridge in our room. Make sure she eats soon;

she's had a rough day."

The soldiers were all supposed to be fed once a day, a far cry from the normal weekly feeding schedule The Elite followed. Being pregnant, Rachel needed the extra blood. With their kind, the more blood they consumed, and the more often they consumed it, the stronger they became. That was why Martinez's mission was so crucial. Infected vampires were practically insatiable, usually feeding as often as they were able to find blood, which only served to boost their already-superior strength. The Elite needed blood, a lot of blood, if they were going to stand a chance in the fight ahead.

Martinez waited while his men filed through the entrance of the tunnel, each rolling an empty cart behind them to transport their haul from the other side. Grabbing his cart, he looked over and caught a glimpse of Captain Erikson hovering around the corner but, as they'd agreed, he didn't acknowledge his presence and instead simply followed behind his men.

Reaching the other end of the tunnel, Martinez was the first to exit, casting a concealing mist over himself before he did. Using his ability on such a small scale, and only creating a visual block, was much less taxing than casting a full concealment, thus allowing him to focus on the task at hand. He surveyed the area, noting the sounds of sirens and screaming off in the distance, evidence of the abductions he'd learned about back on the compound. Luckily, the area surrounding the secret entrance to the tunnel was abandoned and it was only a couple of blocks to the meeting point where Davies would be waiting. Martinez dropped the veil and signaled to the rest of his team, all of whom were behind him in an instant. The group moved silently through the night, sticking to the shadows and using only back alleys to reach their destination where, as expected, they found two unmarked carrier vans which, though they knew better, appeared to be abandoned.

Martinez halted the team and dropped a fresh layer of mist as he approached the driver's side door of the priority van. He lifted his cover and gave the door three steady taps to signal that they had arrived. The locks immediately disengaged.

"Right on time," Davies said, stepping out from between the vans. Martinez had never met the man, but he wasn't quite what he'd been expecting. The Commander's brother-in-law was clean-cut and very well dressed. He reminded him more of a tax accountant than a drug dealer, which is essentially what he was by vampire standards. "The keys are in the other one already," he said, passing a set of keys to Martinez as the rest of the team appeared out of the darkness.

A nearby truck started. "We'll be right behind you until you're back through," he said before flashing to the truck where his men were waiting. Martinez slid into the driver's seat of the van and was joined by one of his men up front, while another climbed to the roof. The remaining team members repeated the configuration with the other van before they drove away. Luckily, the alleys they'd used to travel to the pickup point were wide enough to accommodate the vans on the trip back. This allowed them to return unseen.

They backed both vans up as close to the tunnel entrance as was possible in order to proceed with unloading. When Martinez pulled the door open, he was greeted with a rather nervous smile from a beautiful red-headed woman he knew to be Mrs. Claesson. Though she didn't need it, Martinez offered his hand as she climbed down silently, followed by Ella, Commander Claesson's daughter. None of them spoke, knowing it was best if the pleasantries waited until they were safely behind the protective barrier. When one of the men opened the tunnel entrance, the two women moved through with the speed and grace of their kind. The group made quick work of the stacks that filled the vans, piling box after box of bagged blood onto the carts, while Davies and his men kept watch.

When the last box was loaded, Martinez turned to Davies and offered his hand. "You have our gratitude," he said as the other man returned the gesture. "Just tell Alek to take care of my little sister and—

Martinez swiveled, hearing the shot just before a bullet sliced through the meaty part of his thigh. Fire flashed from an alley across the way as more shots rang out. Davies and his crew took cover and returned fire while The Elite shoved the last cart into the tunnel, using it for cover as bullets tore through some of the boxes and sent blood flying. Martinez tried to stand, yelling out as pain like he'd never felt radiated from his wound. A soldier sped out under the cover of Davies's fire, tossed Martinez over his shoulder, and flashed back into the tunnel.

"Seal the door!" Martinez groaned with everything he had, feeling confused and disoriented as the other soldier set him down and he collapsed under his own weight.

"Something's not right; he should be healing," one of them said as Mrs. Claesson sped over.

"Oh, no," she said, inspecting the wound. "I think he's been infected."

One of the men pulled the slide on his gun and inspected the round in the chamber. "Move back," he said, aiming the weapon at Martinez.

"What the hell are you doing?" Mrs. Claesson demanded, stepping in front of the gun.

"These rounds are tipped with the antiserum. If I shoot him, it should stop the infection, right?"

"I don't know, but there has to be another way to get it to him," she said, looking at Martinez, who was writhing in pain.

"Do it!" he gritted out from behind her.

"Mrs. Claesson, you and Ella need to get out of here. The Commander will have all of our heads if we let you stay for this. Hall, Brandt, grab your carts and lead them back," the soldier said, leveling his gun at Martinez again. "Go!" he shouted when they didn't move.

A single shot reverberated through the tunnel as they disappeared around the bend.

"Get him to the medical wing and get that bullet out before it heals! It's lodged in his femur by the looks of it and it won't come out on its own. It will give him problems for the rest of his life if we leave it," Commander Claesson ordered. He'd barely had a second to hug his wife and daughter before the rest of the team came bursting out of the tunnel with an injured Martinez in tow. Luckily, the antiserum round had done its job and stopped the infection. If it hadn't worked, Martinez would have transitioned before they could get him back to the compound. And though they would have been able to cure him eventually, he would have likely done some serious damage to the blood rations and his fellow soldiers in the meantime.

The men carried Martinez off and the Commander turned his attention back to his family. He opened his arms and both women rushed to him. "I've missed you both."

"We've missed you, too, Daddy," Ella whispered against his chest while he stroked her auburn locks. After holding them for a few moments, he took a step back, an apology already on his lips when Mrs. Claesson stopped him.

"You don't need to apologize. There will be time for us later; you have business to take care of," she stated matter-of-factly. She knew her husband, and his job, well. She had long ago accepted that The Elite were his family as much as she and their daughter were. Knowing how important his role was, she couldn't believe there was anyone alive who could fulfill the duty better than Alek Claesson. It was part of why she loved him. "We know our way around, so we'll see you when you're finished here," she added, taking her daughter's hand and leading her away.

Claesson smiled at their backs, recognizing how lucky he was. It took a special and very strong woman to put up with the kind of life a man like him could offer, always coming in second behind his duty. Eva Claesson did it with more class and grace than he could have ever imagined.

✧

"What about that other issue we discussed? Did he get back in?" Commander Claesson asked.

"I was a little occupied when we sealed the door, but no way. I got hit, and then they dragged me in, and shut the door within seconds. There's not a chance in hell he slipped by unnoticed. Not with Davies and his men in a firefight just outside the door," Martinez replied while Rachel watched curiously.

"Hmm, all right then. I'll leave you to it. Get some rest; it's going to be one hell of a day. Take care of him, Rachel," the Commander said before exiting.

"What was that all about?" she asked, still looking after the Commander.

"To be honest, I'm not sure I even know. Captain Erikson wanted to sneak out when we went to the city. He said it was to contact family, because of the blackout. When I told the Commander, he ordered me to let him. All I know is that the Commander has never trusted the guy and he thinks he's up to something. I guess now we'll find out. He's stuck outside, but he'll be able to get in contact when he's ready to come back. *If* he comes back, I wouldn't want to be him when he tries to explain himself."

"So much for it being an easy supply run," Rachel said, swiping at the tears that started flowing again.

"Don't start that again! Look, I'm totally fine; good as new," he said, flexing his leg back and forth on the bed located in one of the surgical suites of the medical wing. It had only taken a few minutes for the doctor to cut out the infection-laced bullet, and even less time for the wound to heal once Martinez got a couple bags of blood in his system.

"Shut up! I know. It's just hormones, I can't help it."

"Think how crazy the baby's going to make you in a few months," Martinez said, squeezing her hand affectionately. "I can't wait to see you waddling around the compound."

Rachel laughed. "God, can you imagine?"

"Actually, I can't," Martinez said, his tone serious. Her chin quivered as she looked at him. "No, don't cry. Just come here." He pulled her onto bed. "It's just tonight, seeing Commander Claesson and his family. Rach, I don't want that for us; only seeing you who knows when, not being able to hold you every night. I don't think I can do it."

"Oh, John!" she sobbed, bursting into tears again. "What choice do we have? We can't raise the baby on the compound."

"Shh, we've got some time to figure it out. Everything is about to change out there. It might not be so hard if we both leave."

"You would do that?"

"Of course. I would do anything for you and junior," he said, palming her belly.

"It could be a girl, you know," she said, poking him in the side.

"We can still call her junior," he teased, pulling her close and kissing her hair. "No matter what happens, I'll do whatever it takes to be with you, Rachel. I promise."

She buried her face in his chest trying, rather ineffectively, to hide her tears while she nodded her understanding.

"Your blood test came back fine; you're free to leave whenever you're ready, but I'd hurry if I were you. The broadcast will be starting soon and I've heard it's going to last a while. There's a TV a couple of rooms down if you want to stay," the doctor who'd operated on Martinez said as he walked past.

"What do you say, babe? Ready to go watch a little history in the making?"

CHAPTER 16 - *Let There Be Light*

Alexa looked around her parents' suite and sighed. She was surrounded by family, both hers and Ethan's, but one vital person was missing. Chloe.

"Father, something has been bothering me," she said, looking to William. "In your announcement, about the antiserum..." she began.

"Just a little misinformation," William replied, knowing what she was going to ask. "It was Claesson's idea. He's still confident that there is a traitor on the compound. In fact, we're counting on it to get Chloe back. Giving the false information serves two purposes. It keeps the attention from the true source of the antiserum, and it will tell us if

Lucias does, indeed, have a spy. If he learns the location, he'll attack the factory as soon as possible. Our best guess is that he'll do it tomorrow night, considering the fact that it will be dawn in just a few hours. When he does, we'll be ready."

"How can you be so sure he'll attack?"

"His plans have always depended on two things; his virus, and Chloe. Those men do not fight out of loyalty; they fight because he has taken their ability to choose. If we give that back to them, he will lose control of his army and, by extension, Chloe. Lucias is no match for her without an army of men behind him; so rest easy, we'll have our girl back soon. But let us worry about that later. Tonight is about the human integration protocols. This is a historic day for our people."

Alexa wanted to press further, but sensed that it wouldn't do much good. It was comforting to hear that a plan to draw Lucias out was in motion. She couldn't help wondering if it would lead to the meeting of the two armies Josephine had seen in her vision. If that was the case, Chloe would be there.

"Do not worry, Amor," Ethan whispered in her ear, feeling her anxiety through their connection. "I know your father is right; we will have her back soon."

"How much longer do we have to wait for this broadcast?" Jared chimed in, feigning impatience. "Let's get this show on the road; I've got places to be," he teased, trying to lighten the mood though he was telling the truth. He had big plans for the evening, but one of the benefits of being a telepath was that he always knew when a change of subject was in order.

"I'm not sure how to feel about this," Alexa said. "I only found out about vampires a couple of months ago myself. I kind of liked being special, being part of such a big secret. Now it will just be common knowledge," she joked, leaning back into Ethan as she tried to relax. "You will always be special, Amor," he added while softly stroking her forearm. Alexa tilted her head back, earning her a chaste kiss.

"So, do we know who's going to be speaking?" Cami asked. Everyone turned to William.

"Of course Dad knows," Jared replied. "He just won't say."

"Why not?" Elijah asked, leaning forward from his spot beside Josephine.

"Dramatic effect," the High Commander replied with a smirk, and winked at his daughter. *You will see in just a moment; be patient, my children.* he sent to Jared and Alexa.

"It's starting," Rebecca said with the remote in hand. She turned the volume up several notches as a "Breaking News" banner scrolled across the bottom of the large flat-screen. She flipped to several channels, finding the same on each.

"It will be airing on every channel," William stated, "and in every country."

A news anchor for the network came on camera for a moment before the shot cut to a familiar scene.

"Oh, my God! No way!" Alexa said, scanning the room with wide eyes.

An instant later, the room fell silent as the President of the United States took his seat and began to speak.

They all remained glued to the screen as he spoke to the country, seriously and openly, about a subject most believed to be pure fantasy and make-believe. Over the course of nearly four hours he, with the aid of other well-known politicians and several celebrities, laid everything about vampires out on the table, so to speak; separating fact from fiction and offering his reassurance that the average vampire didn't represent any sort of threat to humans. And then came the bad news; Lucias and his army of infected who had been wreaking havoc in Massachusetts and other parts of the world for centuries.

"These infected," the leader of the free world continued, "they are what nightmares are made of and they are why, at the risk of their own safety and way of life, the vampire race has chosen to step out of the shadows. To share with all of us secrets that have been kept for centuries, so that we may fight to protect our way of life, our homes, and our families. And in this fight, we have a powerful ally, one who knows this enemy and will do whatever it takes to see him neutralized."

He continued to announce a partnership between The Elite and the armed forces of which he was Commander-in-Chief; a mutually beneficial arrangement that would provide human soldiers with vital training and enable them to fight alongside The Elite.

"I know many of you will have reservations about our new allies, but I say to you honestly, I have the utmost faith in their integrity and ability. I do not place that faith on a whim, but rather from years of experience in working with, and being protected by, the people I'm asking you all to trust. Vampires have shown themselves to be loyal and dedicated friends by serving as members of not only my Secret Service detail, but those of countless other presidents over many years." The camera panned out to show the lines of Secret Service agents standing on either side of the room.

As the broadcast continued, a new set of vampire-related laws were set forth, which had apparently passed secretly at various times over the years as part of other bills, and a branch of government specifically tasked with handling human-vampire relations was announced. At the end, he acknowledged the expectation of a lot of confusion and uncertainty, for both humans and vampires, in the coming months, but stressed his utmost confidence in the ability of the citizens of his great country, and the world, to move forward with dignity, understanding, and compassion.

Everyone remained silent for a few moments after the broadcast ended and the network went back to whatever late-night show was on at four o'clock in the morning.

"I can't believe that about the Secret Service," Alexa finally said. "Does that mean all those presidents knew all along?"

"Indeed, the information was passed along to every man to take the office. For some it wasn't news, considering the fact that they were vampires themselves," William said proudly.

"You can't be serious!" Alexa said with shock. William simply nodded. "And this one?" she asked.

"He's not," William replied, "but the First Lady is."

"Shit," Alexa said with awe. "But wait, they have children. How is that possible? I thought humans and vampires couldn't conceive with each other."

"It doesn't happen often," Ethan replied. "Most of our kind have avoided mating with humans, but a vampire female can conceive with a human male."

"So, what about the children?"

"They will be vampire as well."

Alexa remained silent for a moment, pondering how much she still didn't know about her own people. Even though she'd believed herself to be one for most of her life, she couldn't imagine how humans around the world were feeling after hearing the truth.

"Maybe it's just me, but I still can't get over Tom Cruise. Did anyone else think it was funny that they used an actor who played a vampire to talk about our history?" Jared opined with a smirk. "It was probably one of his easier roles, considering he's one of us," William replied.

Both Alexa and Jared's jaws dropped. "Shit, I can't believe you never told me that, Dad. You know I loved that movie."

"So why didn't he say as much? Like the Secret Service?" Alexa asked.

"While we are openly sharing our existence, everyone involved has agreed that, for the time being, civilian vampires should not go out of their way to reveal themselves. We expect a fairly positive response from humans as a whole, but there will be groups who are intolerant and will perhaps resort to violence. It is part of, for lack of a better term, human nature. The last thing we need is for a civilian vampire to injure a human in self-defense," William answered. "Now, while I know this has all been rather exciting, it will be dawn soon. We should all try to get some rest. It is going to be a long and important day."

"The world will never be the same," Jared said as he and Cami made their way back to his room.

"I've never spent much time around humans. I imagine it will remain business as usual here on the compound."

"Maybe for the next few hours, but based on what I could see from my father's thoughts, we could very well be at war by the time the sun goes down."

"Like I said; business as usual," Cami replied, opening the door.

"This is different, Cami. It's not going to be the occasional battle with a couple dozen soldiers or secret missions to clean up after the infected. You heard what Father said to Alexa. They expect Lucias to attack the factory tonight."

Of course she knew it was different. As a ranking officer, she'd been party to the plans to draw Lucias out, but on the Commander's orders, none of that information was to be shared, not even with her family or Jared, until he was certain about Lucias's spy.

"You don't need to worry. The Commander knows what he's doing."

"How can I not worry when the future is so uncertain?" he asked, pulling her close.

"The future is always uncertain, Jared," she said, looking up at him through her lashes. He grasped one of her long curls between his fingers, pulled it down, then released it, letting it snap back into place. He loved her hair. She usually kept it pinned up, but now, whenever she wasn't training, she left most of it down just for him.

Jared desperately wanted to make one piece of their future definite. He swallowed hard, suddenly nervous as he considered how to proceed. He knew Cami loved him, but they had only known each other for such a short time and her father had warned him that her ideas about mates and marriage were far from traditional.

He opened his mouth to speak, but before the words left his lips, she silenced him with a demanding kiss.

"I don't want to worry about the future right now, Jared," she panted when she broke away. "I just want to think about right here and right now."

Disappointment flashed in his eyes and she noticed. "What is it?" she asked.

"Nothing; I guess I'm just tired," he replied, lowering his head and pressing a soft kiss to her lips. She leaned into him and desire simmered between them, but she could still tell that something was bothering him. Then it hit her. He'd been acting strangely with her since he'd asked to speak privately with her father.

She smiled against his mouth and kissed him harder. For her whole life, the thought of marriage had made her cringe. Thinking of it with Jared, of being bound to him in such an intimate and unbreakable way, awakened a sense of hope and longing unlike anything she'd ever felt. She wanted it, and not on some far off day in the future. Her heart was screaming now.

Jared gripped her waist and pulled her closer, deepening their kiss, but Cami pulled back suddenly. He looked down at her, his eyes burning with lust and a hint of confusion.

She stared up at him, searching his eyes with her gaze, feeling so full of emotion she thought she would burst. "I want to be bound to you, Jared. Complete the mate bond with me now. Marry me."

It wasn't so much a question, as a demand. His eyebrows knitted together as he tried to understand. He searched her eyes for what felt like a lifetime to her.

"You're so fucking pushy," he growled, finally and crushed his mouth to hers. By the way he kissed her, she had her answer. Jared pulled her legs up around his waist and, in a flash, they were on the bed. A blur of tangled limbs sent their clothes flying. Jared nudged her legs apart and settled in between with his hard length pressing against her sensitive flesh.

"Are you sure?" he groaned out as he settled onto one arm and fought against the urge to push inside her. She responded by taking his other arm, turning her head, and sinking her fangs into his wrist. She kept her eyes pinned on his as his blood filled her mouth and he pushed his throbbing cock inside her. He licked up the length of her exposed neck and felt a shiver travel through her body, his mouth feeling full with the fangs that seemed to have dropped lower than he'd known was possible. Her vein rose to his call, making it impossible to resist any longer. The first taste of her blood mixed with his sent a new wave of sensation through both of their bodies as they became one in the most intimate of ways; every stroke, every caress, the exquisite fire of Cami's climax building. All of it flowed between them as their blood linked them together forever.

When Cami's orgasm washed through her body, it was impossible for Jared to hold on and he fell over the cliff of ecstasy right along with her. They both cried out as wave after wave of pleasure coursed through their bodies and their newly-formed bond. When the intensity of it all finally waned, Jared collapsed beside her and she cuddled up against his side. She touched her neck where the twin punctures burned with pleasure and realized they were still open, as were those on Jared's wrist. Hooking her leg over Jared's hips, Cami straddled him and pulled his wrist to her mouth, keeping her eyes locked on his as she swiped her tongue over the two marks. Jared growled as he watched and his eyes fell to the little trail of blood flowing down her neck and onto her breast. He sat up and wrapped his arms around her back as he licked over the punctures in her neck and ever so slowly followed the trail down until it was all gone.

They stayed there with her on his lap, their faces only inches apart, as they stared into each other's eyes.

"I love you, Camille."

"I love you, Jared."

✧

Lucias's roar shook the room before the remote crashed into the screen, shattering it completely.

Molly sat completely still, almost afraid to even breathe. She knew Lucias, perhaps better than anyone, and she'd seen him angry many times, but there was always a sense of control in it. What she was seeing was something else entirely. Like a rabid dog trapped in a corner, and perhaps for the first time since the night she met him, she feared for her life, knowing that the slightest provocation could incur his wrath.

He moved to the window and stared out into the darkness, remaining there for the longest time without saying a word, before he finally turned to Molly.

She carefully schooled her features and returned his gaze.

"I must admit, this," he said flicking his hand towards the shattered television, "was unexpected."

Molly let out a breath, seeing that he had regained control.

"What does it mean?" she asked carefully.

"Merely that we must be more cautious, but it also tells me The Elite have become desperate. The Agency recognizes my power. They know Claesson and his men cannot defeat me on their own, so they have turned to the humans for aid. There has been no movement around the compound so far, but they will bring human soldiers here. Fools. The Elite mean to use them as a shield to distract my men. They think if they have enough bodies they can overwhelm my army. But they know nothing of you, my pet, or the hundreds of others like you. They are going to bring thousands of highly- trained human soldiers right to my doorstep; mine for the taking," he said with a sneer. The broadcast had enraged him, but the longer Lucias thought and the longer he talked, the more confident he felt that he would be able to use The Agency's plan against them.

Molly smiled and stood to make her way over to him. She needed to keep up appearances, after all. Before she reached him, however, there was a knock at the door.

An expression of irritation spread over Lucias's face. He flashed to the door and yanked it open. "You had better have an excellent excuse for disturbing me at this hour," he hissed at the infected standing in the hallway.

"Yes, Sire. There is a soldier at the gate. He claims to be a friend of yours, but I have never seen him before."

Without responding, Lucias sped to his desk and pulled up the security feed for the front gate. A wide smile spread across his face. "Bring him to me immediately," he ordered. "Unharmed," he amended.

Molly watched with curiosity and suspicion as the two men embraced for a strangely long time.

"Christopher, what have you done?" Lucias said finally stepping back, but keeping his hands on the other man's shoulders.

"I had to come. I was almost caught getting my last message to you and still it took me days to get it out. The information I have now couldn't wait," the man said nervously, his eyes moving to Molly for the first time. "Did you see the announcement? The humans know about us now."

"Yes, I was watching. You can speak freely in front of her. Molly, this is Christopher Erikson, my oldest and most dedicated friend," Lucias said, his tone bordering on pride. Looking at the pair, it was obvious there was a great deal of affection between the two men.

"It's nice to meet you, Christopher," Molly drawled, her tone dripping in sweetness.

"Molly is very special to me Christopher, I would like very much for the two of you to get better acquainted, but first you must tell me what is so important you would risk revealing yourself."

"The virus, The Elite have found a cure."

Lucias's stare snapped to him, his expression one of disbelief. "That's not possible," he stated breathily.

"It is true. The two infected you sent to the compound; they are no longer yours. I heard it from the High Commander's lips that his daughter's husband was cured and later, before the broadcast, he spoke to the entire compound announcing they had developed an antiserum."

If Molly thought Lucias seemed out of control after watching the President reveal the truth of their kind, it was nothing compared to what she saw in him now. He didn't let it show in his demeanor, but it was in his eyes, which went as black as night, like two pools of pure hate.

"What else did you learn, how much of this antiserum do they have?" Lucias pressed as he struggled to compose himself again.

"Not much from what I can tell, but they have set up a laboratory outside of town to manufacture it around the clock. They expect to have enough for what they estimate to be your entire army within a week."

Lucias ran a hand through his hair and began to pace, an uncharacteristic display of his anxiety over the news.

"You see why I had to come? But I have good news as well. I know the precise location of the lab," Erikson said moving closer to Lucias whose expression immediately changed.

"That is good news. Do you know how many men guard it?"

"I wasn't able to gather any further information. The compound has been on lockdown with all communications restricted since we arrived. I was only able to get out by sneaking through with a team on a supply run. It seems their blood rations have all but run out, forcing Commander Claesson to enlist the services of a blood dealer in the city. As soon as I got away from the team, I drew a group of infected to their location, so it is possible they weren't able to get the shipment back, but I can't be certain."

"Ahh, so I have you to thank for that? My men reported a run-in with The Elite, but they were unable to stop them. It seems an Elite soldier was injured in the fray and I was quite pleased to learn he'd been infected, but I imagine they will be able to cure him now. How disappointing, but no matter, we will take care of this cure. I still have a few tricks up my sleeve. Isn't that right, Molly?" Lucias said with a smirk.

The Elite might have a cure, but they didn't know Lucias could turn humans and had already accumulated two-hundred new soldiers with a hundred more awaiting transformation, all of which he planned to infect shortly. He would send Molly and Christopher to scout this laboratory during the day and when night fell they would make short order of The Elite's last hope.

CHAPTER 17 - *Ready Your Arms*

"Even though I'm looking at you, I still can't believe it," Erikson said, cutting his gaze to Molly in the passenger seat. Learning that humans could be made vampire, and that the man he loved was in control of the only source of that power, let him know that he'd made the right choice in abandoning his previous assignment. Once the cure was destroyed, they would have everything they'd ever dreamed of.

The black SUV rolled up to a stop sign on the country road that ran parallel to the location of the Adam's shoe factory. Since neither Molly nor Erikson was infected, and Lucias actually trusted both of them despite that fact, he'd tasked them with the daylight assignment of scouting the lab where the antiserum was being produced.

"I can hardly believe it myself," Molly replied with a smile. "It is an amazing gift; I owe Lucias everything," she lied. Her allegiance was to Chloe alone. That allegiance was the only thing that allowed her to put on a convincing act with Lucias. She'd been reluctant to leave Chloe, concerned that without her there to distract him, he would attempt to get Chloe into his bed. Fortunately, there were a hundred humans waiting to be turned, which provided more than enough of a diversion. Lucias had demanded that Chloe spend the morning doing just that while some of his men were tasked with infecting those who had already completed the transformation.

"How much farther is—" Molly stopped when her preternatural sight answered the question for her.

"Oh, no," Erikson said slowing the vehicle. They could see the building they were looking for off in the distance, but that wasn't what had caused them to pause. Stretching the entire length of the field up to the tree line and surrounding the lab was a massive Elite camp. From the looks of it, Erikson would have guessed that over half of the compound was present, maybe more. "We can't get any closer without the risk of being caught," he said, turning onto a side road.

He pulled off, parking the car behind the cover of some trees and stepped out, leaving the engine running. Quickly scanning the area with his senses for signs of anyone, human or vampire, he pulled a camera with a telephoto lens from the bag in the backseat. He moved just far enough beyond the trees to snap photos of the entire camp before rushing back to the vehicle.

"I didn't expect them to move this quickly. All of these soldiers were still on the compound last night," he said, turning the car back onto the road.

"So what does this mean?" Molly asked.

"It means we're going to war."

✦

"What's going on with you?" Jackson asked with one eyebrow cocked. "You look like the cat that ate the canary."

"Nothing; I'm just in a good mood," Cami replied, trying, and failing miserably, to wipe the smile off her face.

Just then Commander Claesson stormed into the pit.

He looked around at his first-in-command and the ranking officers from the other compounds. Satisfied that all were in attendance, he took a seat.

"It's been one hell of a night," he began. "I just spoke with Esther and they managed to get everything set at the old factory just after dawn, but we have another problem. Martinez was shot during last night's blood run, and it looks like that bastard Lucias has started lacing his ammunition with the virus. That means that every one of our soldiers is going to have to get a shot of antiserum before we head out. As it stands, if you take out the doses we'll need for our people, we're only going to have enough antiserum rounds for about two-thirds of the infected, give or take, depending on how good our aim is."

"Can't we just make more?" one of the officers asked.

"That's not an option; at least, not by tonight. There's still a chance that we'll have some more time, but we need to plan as if we don't. I want the bulk of the antiserum rounds with the snipers; load everyone else up with silver and tranquilizer rounds. The Agency wants us to try to save as many as we can without risking ourselves.

"So what happens if no one shows up at the factory today?" Cami asked, pushing a stray curl back from her face.

"We'll have to find another way to draw him out, or wait for him to come to us. Either way, at most we'll have another day. He's not going to risk giving us the time to get thousands of more soldiers from the human military here after last night's big reveal. My money is on him showing up tonight, so let's go over the plan again," Claesson continued, pulling up the map of the factory and surrounding area.

"I want the snipers positioned at these vantage points," he began, pointing to several markers, "Cami, your—

"Sorry to interrupt, Commander," Jester said, bursting in, "but we just got the call you were expecting."

"And?"

"A black SUV with two passengers drove within range and took photographs of the area. The passenger was a blonde woman and the driver who took the shots, fucking Erickson."

"You're sure?" Claesson asked.

"One-hundred percent; the scout team took some photos of their own," Jester replied, turning his laptop around to show the Commander.

"Well, damn. Looks like we're on for tonight as planned. I knew that son of a bitch was up to something! Cami, take over for me here for a few minutes. I need to report to the High Commander. I don't want him hearing this from someone else. This is going to be hard on him; Erikson has been with him for as long as I can remember."

"Yes, sir. Does this mean we can fill our men in on what's going down tonight?"

"Absolutely; when we're finished here we need to start rounding everyone up to administer the antiserum. We can tell them then."

"And what about the civilians on the compound?" Cami pressed, knowing it was going to be impossible to continue to keep it a secret from Jared for much longer. Completing the blood bond made it that much easier for him to read her, which is why she'd slipped out of bed for the meeting without waking him.

"After we tell the men."

"Then this will be where The Elite will make their final stand," Lucias said, as he looked over the pictures Captain Erikson and Molly had presented, "and it will be the last time they resist me." Lucias moved to the chair behind his desk. "My civilian resources have informed me that the first round of human soldiers will be arriving tomorrow; too late to do The Elite much good, but excellent timing for us. Christopher, you are certain about the number of soldiers The Elite have in Boston?"

"Yes, Lucias, I'm absolutely certain. I was able to get a count of Elite stationed at the compound from Claesson's office and I have been diligent in tracking the new soldiers arriving each day. Just a little over three-hundred-and-fifty have come from the other compounds. That brings their total to around six-hundred men."

Lucias smiled. "It is going to be a short battle. My army of infected alone is nearly double that number and that is saying nothing of the turned humans. Of course, they are not yet trained, but being newly infected, their bloodlust will make up for the lack of skill in battle. Molly, I want you to go see to Chloe. Give her a little incentive to finish the transformations quickly."

"What kind of incentive?" Molly asked with a devious smile. She was an excellent actress.

"Inform her that if every one of the humans is not ready for infection within the hour, she'll have the pleasure of watching Kaleb tear the throats out of any who remain human."

Molly gave a slow nod and disappeared through the door.

"Come, Christopher; let us go and see the new additions to my army. It has been so very long since you've seen my virus in action. I have made some rather entertaining modifications over the years. It is truly

241

a magnificent sight to behold." Lucias offered his arm, which the other vampire happily accepted, and the pair sped off.

✧

"What do you mean it's not working?" Lucias hissed, inches away from Mason's face.

"Sire, I don't know what's wrong," Mason replied anxiously. "I've given each of them three shots and nothing has happened."

Lucias sped over to one of the new vampires and grabbed the dark-haired man by the throat. "How do you feel?" he asked, eyeing the man carefully.

"Amazing. What did you do to me?" There was fear in his eyes, but something else as well; gratitude, admiration.

Lucias released his hold and thought for a moment before responding. "I have given you a gift. Lifted you far above all of those you once knew. Before, where you were just a man, now you will be a god. In return for this gift, you must pledge your allegiance to me and earn your place. Will you do this?"

"Yes, anything," the man replied without hesitation. Lucias looked back at Christopher, who was watching with curiosity before he turned to address the nine other vampires who'd been silently observing. "And what of the rest of you; do you accept this gift and pledge your allegiance to me?" Like the first, every one of them agreed without hesitation. Lucias watched them all carefully; he listened to their hearts beating, but detected no lie. Apparently, humans were far more pliable than he'd realized.

"Mason, take our new guests," he said gesturing to the turned, "and gather the others in the main hall to await my arrival. I will be there shortly to speak with all of them."

"Yes, Sire," he responded and, before he even asked, the other vampires filed in behind him.

"How marvelous," Lucias said, turning to Christopher after they left the room. "It seems these turned are as obedient and loyal as the infected."

"Are you sure they will be able to fight?" Christopher asked.

"It matters not. They increase my forces by three-hundred, even if only to occupy The Elite, forcing them to waste whatever antiserum they possess while we destroy the lab. And they can easily be replaced. Now, my dear Christopher; I think it's time for you to get reacquainted with an old friend."

"Here, you must drink," Molly said, passing a bag of blood to Chloe who was slumped on the floor. The last of the humans had been carted off to complete transformation several minutes before. Completing the task in such a short time had left Chloe drained, especially since she hadn't drunk nearly as much blood as she should have during the process.

Chloe looked up at her with tears on her lashes. "He's never going to stop; he'll never let me stop. Maybe it would be better if I died; then The Elite would still have a chance."

"Don't talk like that, Chloe. Without you, we would be lost," she said, kneeling down to comfort her maker. "We need you, and your family needs you now more than ever. I have something to show you, but you must drink first."

Reluctantly, Chloe bit through the plastic and drank down its contents before she pushed into Molly's mind. There she saw Captain Erikson with Lucias and Molly, and then in the car with Molly, and finally outside The Elite camp at the factory.

The Elite have found a cure and Lucias plans to attack them tonight. This man, Christopher, says nearly all of The Elite are guarding the lab we saw this morning. They will be slaughtered; Lucias has so many more men.

Chloe's eyes widened then rolled back into her head as she fell limp in Molly's arms. Molly fought off the panic that threatened to overtake her and gently lowered Chloe to the floor. She rushed to retrieve more blood from a cooler on the other side of the room, assuming that her maker's need for it was the cause of her current state. But before she even made it back, Chloe sat up.

"Oh, my God; are you all right? You scared the shit out of me!" Molly said, her southern accent thicker than ever under the stress of the moment.

"I'm better than all right," Chloe said, taking the two bags from Molly's hands. She was drinking down the last few swallows of red liquid when Lucias, followed closely by Captain Erikson, entered the room.

"Ahh, there you are," Lucias said rather cheerfully at seeing the two women.

"I was just about to come find you," Molly said with a smile, speeding over to him.

"I take it your young charge managed to complete the task as requested." Lucias asked.

"They took the last one outta here about fifteen minutes ago," Molly replied as Chloe, fully recharged, stood up behind her.

"Excellent. Chloe, you remember Christopher, or rather Captain Erikson as you would have known him?"

"Of course; it's a pleasure to see you again, Captain," she replied, schooling her features to hide her disgust. She'd always had a bad feeling around Captain Erikson; now she knew why, but she didn't understand how he could have hidden his betrayal for so long. Her grandfather was an incredibly powerful telepath; surely at some point over all the years Captain Erikson had served him he would have detected something of his true intentions in his thoughts.

As if he'd read her mind, Lucias provided the answer.

"I suppose you must be curious how Christopher managed to elude your grandfather's ability all these years. I must say, it was one of my better ideas, genius really. You see, Christopher is my blood-bound mate," he said, taking the other man's hand.

Neither she nor Molly could quite conceal their shock at that statement or action. Though she found both men utterly repugnant, Chloe caught the tiniest glimmer of goodness in them both through their shared affection.

"Don't look so surprised," Lucias continued. "Through that bond, I was able to command Christopher, to help him repress any thoughts that could jeopardize his mission. Thus, there was nothing for William to detect but his commitment to his duty. But now, thanks in part to you, dear Chloe, there is no longer a need for us to hide."

"I'm happy for you then," Chloe replied and it was, in fact, the truth. The Captain's presence provided yet another distraction to keep Lucias's mind off of her, and with the vision she'd just had, she was fairly certain holding Lucias at bay wouldn't be a concern for much longer.

"Retire to your quarters and rest," Lucias commanded Chloe. "You will need your strength for tonight," he continued, moving with Captain Erikson to take her hand as well. "Come, I think it is time for the two of you to get better acquainted," Lucias murmured as his eyes darkened with desire.

CHAPTER 18 - *Worth Fighting For*

"So that's everything," Cami said with the eyes of her entire family locked on her.

"Oh, my God!" Alexa said, looking to Ethan. "It's really happening."

She turned to her father and the smile melted from her face at seeing his expression.

What is it? Aren't you happy? she sent.

Of course I am, darling. It's just, the Captain. I don't understand how he could do this, after all our years together.

I'm sorry, Father; truly, I am.

He replied with a weak smile.

"We're going to start moving out at noon. That will give us about six hours to get everything in place before the sun starts to go down."

Ethan's glance moved to Alexa and she sighed, knowing what was coming. "I want to go out with you," he said to his sister.

"Ethan, we've already discussed this. You and my daughter have been through enough already, I won't see her hurt again if something happens to you," William replied.

"It's okay, Father," Alexa chimed in. "Josephine, you believe this meeting of the armies is what you saw in your vision, right?" she asked of her mother-in-law while keeping her eyes on Ethan. He watched her curiously.

"Yes, I am now certain it was at this factory."

"Then that means Chloe will be there during the battle. I can't ask Ethan, as a father, to stay behind, knowing that," she continued. Ethan smiled and pulled her into his arms. "But, with that being said, I am Chloe's mother, so he can't ask it of me either."

"Alexa, no!" he said, stepping back from her and grabbing her shoulders.

"Ethan, if you go, my whole world will be out on that field. You can't expect me to stay back here while my fate is decided without me. And

I've given it a lot of thought; I want you to go, I want us to go. All of the soldiers, they are going to have their hands full fighting the infected. I know they will do what they can, but they don't love her. She's our daughter and we will protect her more fiercely than anyone else possibly could."

"Alexa's right," Jared added, stepping closer. "I'm going, too, and don't you dare try to stop me," he said when Cami opened her mouth to protest. "My mate is going, my sister is going, and it's my niece out there."

Everyone, apart from Cami, looked at Jared with shocked expressions. "Oh, yeah," Jared said, running a hand through his hair and flashing a lopsided grin, "we didn't mean to tell you all like this," he started, grabbing Cami's hand and pulling her in front of him, "but we completed the mate bond. It's official. Well, almost official."

Sorry, Father. he sent immediately knowing they'd broken with tradition and the regulations of The Agency by not getting approval first.

"We'd like to complete the ceremony with all of you there when all of this is over," Cami added quickly.

William stepped forward, his face serious as he looked at his son, then Cami, before a bright smile lit his face and he yanked them into a warm embrace. "I couldn't be happier!" he said aloud. *The rest of The Agency doesn't need to know about the timing.* he added silently.

"I think you may have gotten the order of things backwards, son,"

Elijah joked, shaking Jared's hand. "I did warn you that my daughter doesn't exactly like to follow tradition."

"Congratulations to you both," Rebecca said, taking each of their hands before she turned to her husband. "William, I agree with Alexa and Jared. I think we should all go, for Chloe." William began to shake his head, but his wife was having none of it. "Not only that, but it seems the fate of our people may very well rest upon the outcome of this one night. I refuse to stay behind and do nothing. You are our leader and Chloe is our granddaughter."

"She's right," Josephine chimed in. "I'm going, too."

Elijah looked at Ethan, then William, and shrugged. "It appears we have been out-voted."

William sighed up at the ceiling, knowing this was one battle he couldn't win. As the High Commander, he could, of course, force all of them to stay within the safety of the compound, but they would never forgive him, especially if something happened to Chloe.

"Fine," he said, finally relenting, "but we will stay near the Commander and you will all give me your word that you will follow his orders no matter what occurs."

Alexa threw her arms around her mother. A moment later the buzzer at the door sounded.

William opened it and Alexa's face lit up even further at seeing Dante and Layla standing just outside. "I'm sorry to disturb you, my lord,"

Dante began. "We realize you are incredibly busy, but this will only take a moment. We've come to request permission to be wed, to complete the mate bond. In light of what's happening we want to do it today, right now really. The Commander has already given his blessing and an officer from one of the other compounds has agreed to perform the ceremony," he said and smiled down at Layla proudly.

Alexa squealed and rushed forward, throwing her arms around the couple as her father stepped back to let them into the suite.

"There must be something in the water," Elijah said, nudging Jared.

"I'm sorry, Dante, but that plan isn't going to work," William replied seriously. Dante's smile melted. "I'll only allow it if you grant me the honor of performing the ceremony myself, and if we can make it a joint celebration."

Relief and confusion swam in Dante's eyes. "You see, my son and Cami have just told us they would like to be married today as well."

Dante and Layla both looked more than surprised as their gazes shot to Cami and Jared.

"Well, now. Come on, dears," Rebecca said, rushing to Layla while Josephine grabbed Cami, "it seems we have a wedding to plan."

The visiting soldiers continued with preparations for the coming battle while the Boston Elite gathered outside. Commander Claesson felt it only right that his men attend the ceremony since it was two of their own being joined. It may have seemed inappropriate to some to

251

take the men away from their duties for even a moment, but considering that so many of The Elite were without family, living their lives dedicated only to the fight, he believed they needed a reminder of what they were truly fighting for. Something to show them that, despite their pledge to protect the people of their race, there was more out there for them. That they could have love.

He thought it was the least he could do as he looked at his beautiful wife seated next to him.

"This is so wonderful, Daddy," Ella whispered from the seat on his other side. "Do you ever think I'll get married?" she asked, with a hint of sadness in her voice. The Commander's heart squeezed tight. In his desire to keep Eva and Ella safe, his daughter had lived a life that went beyond the definition of sheltered. Not to mention, any man who knew who her father was would have to be legally insane to pursue Ella Claesson.

"Of course you will, baby. After today, things are going to be different," he replied, while silently praying it was true.

"Sir, Esther just called. The other witches will be here soon t—"

Jester stopped cold when his eyes fell on Ella, sitting next to her father. She smiled up at him. "Um, Esther called…"

"You said that already," Claesson said, eyeing him suspiciously, seeing the direction of his gaze. He snapped his fingers in Jester's line of sight.

"Sorry, sir," he said with a goofy grin. "The other witches will be here soon to begin casting the concealment with Martinez."

"Good; thanks, Jester." His gaze returned to Ella, who was looking up at him through her lashes with a slight blush dusting her cheeks. "That'll be all, Jester," the Commander added, with a slight edge of irritation in his tone. He liked Jester, a lot, but he was beginning to rethink his good opinion of him after the way he was looking at his baby girl.

Jester finally got the hint and headed back to his seat at the back of the crowd. He'd set up back there with his laptop, wanting to attend, but needing to continue monitoring what was happening outside. There were mixed reports coming in regarding the human response to the broadcast. There were pro-vampire rallies and celebrations popping up all over the map and a number of hate groups taking form, but nothing more than what The Agency had anticipated and prepared for.

Due to the serious time constraints, the two couples had chosen to forego most of the pomp and circumstance of such an event, but the intricate gardens of the mansion provided an ideal setting nonetheless. The four of them met William at the front of the crowd with the beautiful mansion setting the backdrop as he began to speak in the old tongue.

Ethan squeezed Alexa's hand as they listened to the same words that had been spoken at their own mating ceremony only months before. William moved first to Jared and Cami with the small dagger and red satin ribbon and said the sacred words in English.

"I bind myself to you, Cami; blood, mind, body, and soul. I give myself to you freely and without reservation, to serve you, by my life or my death, from this day into eternity," Jared repeated and took the dagger. Making a small cut in his wrist, he passed the blade to Cami before she spoke the same words and slid the cool metal across her skin. William smiled at them as he joined their bloodied wrists and bound them with the red ribbon as he spoke the final words of the ritual.

"I love you," Jared mouthed silently to Cami, while his father moved to Dante and Layla, repeating the ceremony with them. After their wrists were joined, William stepped back to his place and spoke out to the crowd in the old language.

"Let all those present witness and rejoice in these most sacred of unions," he repeated in English.

"By the blood, we bear witness," the crowd recited as one.

Dante carried Layla over the threshold of their room, having grabbed her hand and disappeared through the crowd before the applause had even died down. He knew that they only had a precious few minutes to complete the mating ritual. After everything Alexa and her family had done to help him save Layla, there was no way he could abandon them as they fought to save Chloe.

He set Layla down on her feet, lowering his head to kiss her, but she flashed away just before he made contact. Dante growled, seeing her already completely naked, standing beside the bed with a hand on her hip. She bit her lip, flashing fully- extended fangs as she crooked her finger at him. Perhaps even faster than she'd done it, Dante stripped off his own clothes and was before her with only a few short inches of space separating them and several thick hard inches pressing against her belly.

He stared down at her, his eyes smoldering with love and desire, and pure unadulterated need. His gaze drifted from her eyes, to her full lips, then lower to the base of her neck, where his vision narrowed on her pulse for two slow beats as his fangs pushed even lower, before traveling to her perfect milky white breasts, and he growled again. Somehow, he managed to remain still, waiting for her to make the first move.

She didn't disappoint. Layla pushed up on her toes and captured his bottom lip between her teeth, her tongue sliding over it as she wrapped her fingers around his cock. Dante groaned at the feel of her finally touching him and his hips thrust involuntarily into her grasp. She released his lip and led him back, still gripping him tight until her legs hit the bed. She sat down and slid back, finally letting go as he crawled with her and covered her body with his. She grabbed his face and kissed him forcefully while he hovered above her with his palms pressed into the bed.

"I love you, Dante," she moaned.

"I love you, Layla, so much," he replied kissing her again. He tried to nudge her legs apart with his knee, but she smiled against his mouth and flipped beneath as she grabbed one of his arms. The rapid motion caught him off guard and he lost his balance coming down on top of her. It seemed that had been her intention as she buried her fangs into the flesh of his wrist. Dante cried out with the pleasure of her bite as she pulled hard on his vein. His hard length throbbed between them and she shifted her hips in invitation. Dante rolled just enough to get use of his free arm and position himself between her legs. She raised her hips as he rubbed against her opening and pushed back against him. He moaned at the feel of her tight body swallowing the head of his erection as he lowered his body, letting his weight push him in to the hilt. Layla cried out against his wrist, but didn't release it, knowing she needed to be drinking his blood when he bit her. Following her lead, Dante pushed her blonde locks to the side, exposing her long neck, before he struck. His eyes went wide as he tasted her for the first time. It was like nothing he'd ever felt as the separate sensations of their bodies melted into one simultaneous feeling. He rocked into her and her body trembled beneath and around him as her sweet essence ran down his throat.

Layla released his wrist and he let go of her neck, giving him the freedom to really move. He slipped one arm beneath her hips and pulled her up to her knees as he marveled at the incredible sensation of feeling her tight walls clenching him, while at the same time feeling her pleasure of being filled by him. As difficult as it was, Dante pulled away from Layla's warmth, wanting to see her face when she found her release, and flipped her to her back. He crushed his mouth to hers as he thrust inside her again and she came apart, the waves of orgasm crashing down on her like a tsunami. It was too much. Dante roared out into the room as her pleasure set off his own climax.

He laid there on top of her as they panted together, relishing the amazing thing that was their bond. Finally he rolled away and sighed. She reached for his lingering erection and stroked him as she kissed his chest. "We must get ready to go and join the others," he groaned. She replied by kissing his cheek and speeding off to the bathroom. He smiled at hearing the shower start as she shouted, "Then we'll have to multitask!"

CHAPTER 19 - *The Battle Begins*

"Take your time, pet." Lucias said, stopping to admire Molly's naked beauty sprawled out on the bed. She smiled lazily and sat up. Christopher was standing behind him, already showered and dressed. Lucias fastened the last buttons on his shirt while Molly crossed to the bathroom.

"The sun will be going down in about an hour. I have decided to accompany my men this evening and I would like very much for you to come and enjoy the victory with us as well."

"I wouldn't miss it," Molly drawled and slipped through the door.

"I understand now why you're so fond of her, Lucias" Christopher whispered against the back of his neck. "She is rather magnificent."

"If you'd like, you can go rest in my private quarters. I have business to attend to with our secret weapon."

"I would prefer to remain by your side. I have spent enough time away from you, Lucias."

"Very well," he replied before they sped down the corridor to the area where Kaleb and Anna were being held.

The two guards outside Kaleb's door moved to make room for Lucias and Christopher. "Retrieve Asana and take her to Chloe's quarters immediately," he ordered one of them, while the other opened the door.

"Follow me," Lucias commanded into the darkness without greeting or even bothering to look at his only living son. He was a tool to force Chloe's obedience, nothing more.

A few minutes later, with Anna in tow, they arrived at Chloe's quarters. Lucias pushed through the door unannounced, not that Chloe needed it. She'd sensed them coming shortly after Asana arrived.

Chloe's heart pounded in her chest as she stared at Kaleb, silently willing him to look at her. Instead, his eyes remained downcast, his expression devoid of any emotion. The same was true for Anna and her mother, who stood helplessly beside Chloe.

"We will be leaving when the sun sets," Lucias began. "The two of you will accompany me, with the understanding that I require absolute obedience." Chloe stared back at Lucias, her expression passive, but there was a fire burning behind her eyes. "To ensure that you don't get any ideas out there, my dear Chloe…" he said, stepping to his son. He placed his hand under his chin and lifted his gaze. "Kaleb, if Chloe fails to follow any command I give from this moment forward, or attempts to harm me in any way, you are to kill Anna and Asana, and then you will take your own life." Chloe gasped behind him and tears of anger filled her eyes. Her power began to rise and she trembled against its force, at once wanting to unleash it on Lucias and hold it at bay.

"There now," Lucias said as if he'd just tidied up a small mess rather than ordered his own son to commit suicide. "Anna, Kaleb, this way," he said, gesturing to the door. "As for you two, be at my door in thirty minutes."

The door clicked shut and Asana crumpled to the floor and began to sob. Fighting against her own emotions, Chloe kneeled beside her and pulled her close, wrapping her arms around her friend's shoulders. "Shh, Asana. He has not won yet," she whispered.

"Have, have you seen what is to come?" Asana stammered through her cries.

"No, but if we do what he says, everything will be fine," Chloe lied aloud to avoid revealing anything to Lucias through his surveillance equipment.

I have seen enough to know hope is not lost. Lucias means to use me to defeat The Elite, but he is foolish, power hungry. It will not be enough to defeat them. He wants to demonstrate the might of his army first; that will be our chance. I promise you I won't let anything happen to you or Anna. I swear it.

"Come; dry your tears, Asana. We must not be late."

I'm scared. Asana said, looking across the space in the back of the limousine to where Anna and Kaleb were seated off to one side. Lucias was directly across from her and Chloe, with Molly and Captain Erikson on either side of him. From the looks of him and his two companions, you'd think they were heading into the city for dinner and a show rather than following an army into battle.

It's going to be fine; just stay close to me. Chloe sent back. She avoided looking at Lucias and Kaleb, not wanting Lucias to see her fear, so she instead let her gaze drift to the front of the vehicle. She'd been shocked to find that the driver was human, but Asana explained that Lucias had a number of loyal humans working for him. She wasn't really sure what motivated them before, perhaps fear; but now with Chloe's ability, Lucias had a lot more to offer them. A quick peek into the man's mind revealed that Lucias had already made him the promise of immortality. It seemed the egotistical vampire couldn't resist showing off.

Chloe could sense Lucias's excitement, and his thoughts were centered on his victory and the grand speech he had planned when he assumed rule over The Elite. He believed a broadcast was in order, like the one The Agency had tried to use against him. Counting on her family's presence in the camp, Lucias had ordered his men to capture the High Commander alive. Using him as a bargaining chip, he would take over The Agency and systematically use their network, his virus, and Chloe to bring the entire world to its knees.

"We're nearly there," Captain Erikson announced, looking out the window. In his earlier mission, he'd managed to devise a route to the facility that would allow the entire army of nearly thirteen-hundred to travel through the country virtually unnoticed. The car rolled to a stop a few miles from The Elite camp where, as commanded, the generals were waiting just inside the tree line.

"The scouts just returned to report that there has been no change since the photographs were taken this morning. We estimate the same number of men and they are fairly exposed, with the exception of the wooded area on the other side of the factory. If they are cowardly enough to flee, many of them could escape that way. It would be impossible for us to send a unit to intercept before the initial strike without detection."

"The priority is the lab," Lucias replied, sliding out of the vehicle behind Captain Erikson. "I want it all destroyed after a sample is acquired." In discussions with the scientist who developed his virus, a man who, like Asana, was forced to serve Lucias to protect his family, he learned that with a sample of the antiserum to work with, they might be able to alter the virus to render it ineffective and perhaps even find the key to why it didn't work on the turned humans.

"Signal to the men; let it begin," Lucias ordered. Mason and the other generals disappeared into the forest. "Kaleb, Anna, you are to remain close to me at all times. Asana, stay with Anna; that will simplify things if Chloe tests me," he continued with a sneer as he stared Chloe down. "And you, my dear, are not to leave my side unless I command you otherwise, understood?"

"I understand," Chloe replied, her expression stoic.

The army broke off into units and headed for the camp; quietly moving as close as possible without being detected. Lucias watched with barely-contained delight as his men approached the unsuspecting camp where Elite soldiers were going about their business completely unaware.

Chloe scanned the area, unsure how much distance her telepathy could cover, but she had to warn them if she could. She was sure she could reach the nearest Elite soldier, but somehow was only met with silence as she zeroed in on him. Something wasn't right. Before she could investigate any further, shots rang out into the night as the first unit of turned humans sped across the distance towards the camp of Elite soldiers. Within seconds, wave after wave of the infected appeared out of the trees and followed.

"This will be over quickly," Lucias said with satisfaction, before speeding off behind the army to get a closer look at the action. Chloe and the others, as commanded, stayed right beside him, running through the night with preternatural speed.

And then the soldiers slowed and stopped. "What's happening?" Lucias asked of no one in particular since they happened to be in a patch of low ground and none of them could see past the wall of infected. There was a cacophony of the infecteds' murmurs as the crowd split and Mason appeared.

"Mason, what the fuck—"

"Sire, they aren't here," he rushed out.

"What do you mean they're not here? I saw the camp with my own eyes!" he spat.

"When the first men reached the edge of the camp, where the trail crosses the field, they just disappeared; everything disappeared; the men, the lights, the equipment, all of it's gone."

"What of the lab? Did you check inside?" Lucias yelled as his anger continued to rise, fueled by his confusion and frustration.

"They wouldn't leave it unguarded," Captain Erikson interjected.

"It could be a trick; an illusion to protect it so they could send their forces elsewhere! How did you not see this?" he screamed, grabbing Asana by the arms and shaking her with each word. "You become less useful by the minute," he said, tossing her to the ground as he attempted to regain control. "Press forward to the building and check inside. The cure is there," Lucias ordered and Mason knew better than to question him.

"Perhaps we should leave; it may not be safe for you here out in the open, Lucias," Christopher said, placing a tentative hand on his shoulder.

"I will see what is inside that building with my own eyes and not a single man will leave here until I do," he stated, his tone calm again; but his rage was a constant undercurrent, simmering just below the surface, waiting to be unleashed.

"It appears you are correct, Sire. The building is sealed tight with what appears to be a highly-sophisticated security system. I didn't attempt to enter and risk setting it off without talking with you," Mason said when he returned through the swarm of infected.

"Excellent," Lucias replied before he sped off on the path through the center of his army. He stopped a couple of yards from the entrance to the building and the others appeared immediately beside him.

Chloe looked around, recognizing the faces of many, if not all, of the humans she'd turned surrounding the area. Lucias's plan had been to send them into the fray first, assuming The Elite would be lacing their ammunition with antiserum, the same as he had done with his virus. As she continued to take in her surroundings, she realized it was more than their faces she recognized.

I've seen this place, she sent to Asana and Molly. Both women looked to her just as flashes of fire sparked from the darkness of the trees around them.

"We will hold until most of them cross," Claesson whispered into his radio, though it was unnecessary with the veil produced by Martinez, which was being amplified and bent by the witches to cover the whole of The Elite forces; the infected wouldn't have heard him if he'd shouted at the top of his lungs. The illusion that enticed Lucias to show up with his entire army was also courtesy of the witches.

Right beside him, Cami carefully watched the first group that had run through the border of the spell as they waited. Something was off about them, but she wasn't quite sure what it was.

"Can you see Chloe anywhere?" Alexa asked Ethan. Cami looked at her brother as his green-gray eyes scoured the crowd and it hit her. Their eyes.

"Commander, look at them, all of those men closest to the building; they're not infected. Look at their eyes."

"Shit. It looks like there are at least a couple hundred civilians down there," he responded, scanning row after row of vampires before he found a set of red eyes. "How the hell did he get that many civilians? I could see a few, but we would have heard about that number before now."

"We have to be missing something," Cami said as the crowd started to part and they slowly advanced toward the old factory. A single man appeared and flashed around the perimeter of the structure before disappearing back down the path he'd cut through the men.

"All right people," Claesson spoke a little louder, wanting to be certain everyone could hear him loud and clear. "We've got friendlies at the front of the crowd, so save the antiserum rounds for the bodies further back. As soon as—" he stopped when Lucias appeared in front of the building, with Erikson right by his side. William growled at the sight of the man he'd once considered a friend. Alexa gasped, seeing

Chloe behind him. Claesson turned to Alexa and the rest of her family as he released the button on his radio. "All of you hang back here until we draw most of the men back from the building. Lucias will want to stay close to cover and he won't let her out of his sight."

They all nodded their understanding. Neither Alexa nor Ethan took their eyes off of Chloe.

"On my signal, I want a layer of antiserum rounds laid down on the back half before we move. When you're out of those, switch to silver. I Tranquilizers only from my position forward; we don't want to risk hitting Chloe or the civilians, and keep the fire concentrated on the infected unless those civilians engage. Snipers hang back and continue with the antiserum rounds until you run out." He looked at Cami. She nodded. "Ready, Fire!"

Infected soldiers down each side of the formation fell as antiserum rounds cut through the crowd. The Elite rushed out from behind the veil, continuing to shoot as the infected started returning fire. The Elite, who managed to avoid the rounds whizzing by, reached the line, having to jump over the writhing bodies of the infected being cured as the gunshots slowed and the clang of steel joined the cacophony of the battle. With all of The Elite being vaccinated against infection, those who were hit with the virus- laced rounds retreated to the cover of the trees while their bodies healed before they returned to the fight.

In the chaos and confusion, the unit of turned humans who had no training or experience in battle moved away from the action to surround Lucias and the others near the building.

"Lucias, we should run," Erikson said, taking his hand, "they will kill us all! Please, Lucias," he begged, trying to pull him away.

"No! This isn't over yet!" he yelled, yanking his hand away. "What are you doing?! Attack! Shoot back into the trees!" he screamed at the newest additions to his army as shots continued to come from the darkness. They looked at him with eyes full of fear and uncertainty. Lucias rushed forward and grabbed one of the men by the throat as he glared around at the others. "I said attack!" he roared, throwing the man into the crowd. The others moved to the sides, some raising their weapons toward the tangle of bodies and steel while others aimed for the tree lines where some of The Elite remained, carefully picking off infected with antiserum rounds.

"NO!" Chloe screamed, and every one of them stopped cold. Lucias swiveled to glare at her, his rage boiling over as he realized that the turned humans were bound to her, and everything he'd spent his life working for began crumbling down around him. Their loyalty to him had been a trick, no doubt a command she'd given them to help lure him into The Elite's trap. A cruel smile appeared on his face at seeing Kaleb turn to Asana and Anna to carry out his last command. As quickly as it appeared, his smile evaporated when Chloe flicked her hands towards Kaleb and he fell to the ground.

"Lucias, please! Before it's too late," Erikson pleaded again, trying to take hold of him. But Lucias was deaf to his pleas, and he zeroed in on Chloe as she knelt beside an unconscious Kaleb. It was all because of her.

Chloe bit into her own wrist as she sat beside Kaleb.

Asana, grab Anna and hold her as long as you can, Chloe sent before speeding over to the two women. She shoved her bloodied wrist against Anna's mouth so fast the infected vampire barely had time to struggle before the first drops of blood wet her tongue. In a flash, Chloe was back beside Kaleb, and she cradled his head and pulled his chin down to let her blood drip into his mouth.

Take Anna and leave, get as far away as you can. The cure is in my blood; just like my mother. You will be safe if you leave.

Thank you, Chloe, Asana sent, before rushing off into the trees with her daughter.

Kaleb began to stir and latched on to Chloe's wrist, drawing hard on her vein before his red eyes popped open. Within seconds, the blue began to bleed back into his irises and Chloe smiled down at him.

CHAPTER 20 - *A Promise Kept*

Ethan and Alexa fought against every instinct to obey Commander Claesson's orders, waiting with their eyes locked on Chloe as The Elite attacked. And then they lost sight of her as the crowd of civilians swarmed toward her and Lucias.

"Just wait; there are too many of them!" Commander Claesson yelled, seeing what the pair intended before they made a move. "Lucias will not risk her; she's too important."

Finally the crowd shifted and she appeared again. They both let out heavy breaths of relief at seeing her, but their focus was pulled away when the civilians raised their weapons and aimed toward the trees where they were hiding. Claesson, Cami, and the rest of the family prepared to return fire, but they held, knowing that they were still concealed by the mist and had the cover of the trees; not wanting to injure the civilians if they could avoid it.

"NO!" Chloe's scream reverberated through the night air and they all watched with wonder as hundreds of vampires stopped cold and lowered their weapons.

Still Ethan and Alexa watched and waited, while Chloe used her power on Kaleb before she disappeared from view again. "We can't wait any longer!" Ethan yelled when Chloe reappeared. Though he saw his daughter go to his enemy's son willingly, it didn't stop Ethan from seeing red when he realized that Kaleb was biting her. Without a word to Alexa or any of his companions, Ethan flashed away, heading straight for them with every intention of removing Kaleb's head for daring to touch Chloe.

No, Daddy, Chloe sent straight into Ethan's mind. He slowed at hearing her sweet voice for what felt like the very first time and then stopped completely when a flurry of images passed through his mind. *I love him.*

Alexa, who'd immediately sped off after Ethan and sensing his anger and fear for Chloe, stopped when the same words and images passed through her mind. As she stood there, a band of infected cut through the civilians heading straight for Alexa, who was so focused on what she was seeing that she didn't notice them coming. In an instant, Cami and Claesson were there and intercepted the group only a few yards from Alexa. The two Elite, while probably the best fighters in the entire force, were no match for five infected. Cami jumped back, swinging each of her twin blades up to block the blows of two

271

infected, but they continued to press down, her arms trembling under the force of their power. She fell back when the two men went flying and quickly jumped back to her feet, seeing Jared and her father standing before the infected who'd nearly bested her. She pulled her sidearm and fired an antiserum round into each of them just as another shot rang out and one of the other attackers fell to the ground behind Claesson. She took aim again, sending her final round at the infected he was battling. He gave her an appreciative nod as the man hit the ground and the cure spread through his veins. Cami swiveled looking for Alexa and felt paralyzed when she realized that one of the men had managed to get by them. He was moving slowly, obviously injured, but she was out of ammo and too far away to reach Alexa in time. The man raised his blade and Cami cried out, the entire scene seeming to pass in slow- motion. Alexa turned just as the man flew back. Layla stood over him with her boot on his chest, pushing against the hole where a round of silver was still lodged, before she fired an antiserum round into his thigh.

Feeling Alexa's fear, Ethan's head snapped around just in time to see Layla take the infected down. He sped to Alexa's side, pulling her into his arms as he scanned her with his eyes. "Are you all right, Amor?"

"I'm fine, thanks to Layla," she said, sending the woman she'd once thought she hated an appreciative smile.

Satisfied that Cami and her family were safe for the time being, Claesson turned to the main battle, ready to join his men in the fight, when he caught sight of Captain Erikson heading for the trees. He was tempted to chase after him, but before he could decide, four members of William's guard flashed out from the veil of mist and swarmed around the traitor. In an instant, Erikson was disarmed and on his knees while the men held him steady. Claesson smiled when William stepped out from the trees, sword in hand as he approached. As much as the Commander would have enjoyed what happened next, his men needed him, so he turned and sped into the heart of the action.

Lucias dropped to his knees, as the image of Christopher's head rolling across the ground burned into his brain. He'd sensed his mate's fear and fled through the crowd of Chloe's vampires to get to him, but he was too late. He stayed there, unable to move, not knowing what to do as the pain and rage seared his heart, turning it black and evaporating any tiny remnants of goodness that may have remained.

Having lost sight of William and his men, he stood and turned, his gaze zeroing in on Chloe as everything else fell away. Nothing else mattered but making her pay for what she'd taken from him.

His rage and focus were so intense that to Chloe it was like he was screaming right in her ear. She knew he was coming before he'd even taken the first step. He knew he was no match for her, but believed that he had the advantage of surprise since she kept her eyes on Kaleb as the curing power of her blood spread through his body and she gave no indication that she was aware of Lucias's intentions.

She'd become quite skilled at focusing her mind blasts and could have easily disabled Lucias, but she remembered something she'd seen in her father's mind the day she left the compound. It was a thought, far back in his mind, that seemed to be playing on repeat. A promise he'd made that haunted him. A promise she intended to help him keep.

She sought Ethan's mind again and pushed into his consciousness. Ethan froze for a moment before his head snapped to Chloe. "Stay with Cami," he said to Alexa and disappeared into the crowd of civilians before she could respond.

Chloe never even looked up, trusting completely in her father's strength and his love.

Lucias was only a few yards from Chloe; his revenge so close he could taste it. But the only thing he tasted was his own blood as he found himself frozen in place. His gaze fell as he tried to understand why his feet weren't carrying him forward. His heart would have stopped, if it wasn't already stopped as Ethan gripped it firmly in the hand he'd plunged through Lucias's back. Ethan yanked his arm back, pulling Lucias's heart with it as Lucias dropped to his knees. Ethan jumped in front of him, satisfied to see that he hadn't yet lost consciousness. He leaned down and hissed, "I warned you that if you touched my wife, I would rip your heart out, you piece of shit."

Lucias started to fall forward as the last signs of life slipped away. Ethan let his heart fall to the ground and unsheathed his sword; spinning around, he swung it up in time with the descent of Lucias's body, cleanly cutting off his head.

CHAPTER 21 - *Moving Forward*

With Lucias's death, all of the remaining infected were freed from the slavery of his bond, leaving all but a few who'd willingly submitted to Lucias's cause confused and disoriented. Most stopped fighting, as the smell of blood surrounding them called to their bloodlust and they attacked the injured or unconscious around them. This made them easy targets for The Elite, and it wasn't long before the entirety of Lucias's army was disabled.

"What will we do with all of them?" Cami asked, walking up to Commander Claesson.

"Those who have been cured will be rounded up for questioning. We need to determine who they are, and where they came from. I would guess that most of them have families to go back to somewhere. We'll take the remaining infected into custody and keep them contained until more antiserum is made to cure them."

"How the hell are we going to take all of them into custody?" Cami asked, looking around at the hundreds of infected on the ground. Some of them who were unlucky enough to take a shot to the head were actually dead, but the bulk of them were simply unconscious as a result of the tranquilizers. "We can't handle this many prisoners."

"I already have it covered," he replied with a smile, as he inclined his head. Cami looked to where he'd indicated to see lines of Hummers and large US Military trucks driving towards them. The Hummers came to a stop and hundreds of soldiers filed out, armed with silver-plated chains and handcuffs. An older gentleman with silver hair jumped down from one of the front vehicles and made his way over.

"Commander Claesson," he said with a salute. "General," the Commander reciprocated. "How much time do we have before these boys start waking up?" he asked, standing at ease.

"I'd say about four hours with the level of sedative we used. As discussed, our men will help with the transport and escort you to the holding facility, just as a precaution."

"We'll start loading them up then," he replied, offering another salute before he walked back to his men.

Cami followed the Commander up to the abandoned factory, where most of her family was waiting with Chloe. "And what about all of them?" she asked as they passed the civilians.

"I don't know what to make of them. We need to find out why they were here," he replied.

"I can explain," Chloe said, speeding over to wrap her arms around Cami, seeing her for the first time since the battle had ended. "Up until a couple of days ago, they were all human."

Both Cami and the Commander looked at her as if she had two heads.

"It's the most remarkable thing," Elijah said, coming up behind his granddaughter. "You remember all of those humans Lucias abducted in the city? These are those people."

"It can't be," the Commander said in disbelief.

"It's my blood; if a human drinks it, they become like us."

"Yes, an amazing and very dangerous ability," William added as he approached. "It could make life rather difficult with the secret of our kind no longer being secret. Many humans would do anything to become one of us, making your blood a very valuable and rare commodity. Rare and valuable items almost always tend to bring out the very worst in people."

"So what are you saying; what can we do?" Alexa asked, taking Chloe's hand. "All of these people already know and they have families; friends who will eventually learn what happened to them. We can't keep it a secret."

"You!" Alexa jumped as Ethan yelled and sped across the grass. Chloe was right behind him when he grabbed Molly and pinned her to the ground. "Daddy, please; let her go. She saved me. I don't know if I ever would have made it through these last days without her." For good measure, she shared the images of all the things Molly had done to keep her protected from Lucias. "Once she became vampire, she changed. I don't know how to explain it."

"I do," Molly added as Ethan loosened his grip. "It's because of Chloe. Her goodness made me good. It's in her blood. She's the one who saved me, even though I didn't deserve it." Shame flashed in Molly's blue eyes as they welled up with tears. "I'm so sorry for what I did to you," she whispered.

"Let her up, Ethan," Alexa said gently, as she came up behind him.

He moved away and Molly stood. "Thank you for helping our daughter," Alexa said, taking Ethan and Chloe's hands, and the three of them returned to their family.

"So what do we do about Chloe and the humans, or the new vampires; I'm not sure what to call them?" Cami asked, bringing the focus back to the problem at hand.

"Returning them to their families is our only option. It's the right thing to do and it will advance the human integration protocols by leaps and bounds, as will our victory here; but there is still the issue of Chloe's blood. She could continue to live on the compound under the protection of The Elite, but she will always be a temptation for many, even those as noble as The Elite."

"There is another solution," Chloe said with an uncertain smile. "Asana had a vision. If I was to complete the mate bond, the power in my blood will be lost."

"If that's true, of course it would solve the problem; but it could be a great many years before you find your mate," William replied.

Chloe's eyes cut to Alexa, then Ethan who was already shaking his head. Chloe flashed away around the corner and returned with a rather nervous Kaleb in tow.

"She can't be serious," Ethan said in exasperation. Alexa placed a hand on his cheek. "My love, it would seem that fate has brought them together. You, of all people, should know better than to fight fate."

Epilogue

"I'm gonna get you!" Chloe shouted as she ran around the corner. Little Jackson squealed with delight and fell down on the ground to be tickled, a desire his favorite babysitter happily obliged.

"Don't let him wear you out too much," Kaleb said, walking up behind her. He wrapped his arms around her waist and kissed the side of her neck. "You're going to need your energy when I get you home," he whispered, running his nose up the edge of her ear.

"Knock it off, you two," Rachel said, walking up from the main area of the compound with Cami.

"Mama," Jackson said, running up to Rachel with his arms out. She scooped him up and tossed him up into the air, earning a fit of giggles in response.

"I can't get over how much he looks like Jackson," Cami said with a sad smile.

"I know, it almost makes me think twice about the concept of reincarnation," she said, planting a big kiss on her son's cheek as she tried to fight back the tears. It had been fifteen months since her twin brother had been killed in the battle at the Adam's factory, but it never seemed to get any easier.

"Dada?" Jackson said, his tone asking a question he didn't quite have the vocabulary for yet. "Dada is still at work, but he'll be home soon." Jackson squirmed in her arms to get down. "Oh, no you don't," she said, snatching him back up as he tried to make a run for it. "I keep telling the Commander that we need to fence off the family housing from the rest of the compound. Jackson has already figured out how to open doors. One of these days he's going to sneak over there and get his mommy into big trouble with daddy," she said, her voice melting down to baby talk by the end.

"I don't know how you do it," Cami said. "It's great that they built the family housing so that you and Martinez didn't have to live separately when he decided to stay; but you staying, too, with this little monster to chase around every minute you're not running drills or helping with training…"

"It's not so bad; Chloe is a huge help, especially when John and I need a little time alone," she said with a wink.

"Yeah, speaking of time alone, I think your babysitter and her husband snuck off."

"He better make it quick; Claesson is expecting him back to work with Jester on that presentation they're giving with the humans next week."

"Who'd better make what quick?" Alexa asked with a yawn as she waddled out into the garden.

"You don't want to know," Cami replied with a laugh. "I wish you would hurry up and let my nephews out of there already. You've looked like you're ready to pop for at least two months."

"Thanks, Cami. That's what happens with twins, but I absolutely love hearing how huge I am," Alexa replied, sticking her tongue out at her sister-in-law as she settled on a bench in the shade.

"Damnit, Cami, what did I tell you about teasing my beautiful wife?" Ethan challenged, coming up the path with Martinez and Jared. He didn't wait for a response; instead he ran straight to Alexa and leaned down to kiss her as if no one was watching, while Jackson ran straight into his father's arms.

"You know, sis, if you keep that up you're going to spend the rest of your life waddling around in this garden," Jared teased as he pulled Cami out of her seat and pressed a more family-friendly kiss to her lips.

"And what would be wrong with that? Have you ever seen a woman more beautiful than my wife is right now?" Ethan said, dropping to his knees to pepper Alexa's belly with kisses.

"Seriously, it's hard to be around you guys sometimes," Jared said with a laugh.

"Pretty soon this will be you," Alexa said pointing to Cami, "and then I'll be the one laughing."

"No way!" Cami said immediately. "We'll leave it to all the rest of you to have the babies and maybe we'll babysit once in a while if we need to be reminded of why we don't want kids," she teased. Alexa just smiled as she studied her brother's face. Cami might have thought they were on the same page about not wanting children, but Jared's eyes and thoughts told a very different story. At least he had a really, really long time to persuade her to change her mind.

"We should get going," Jared said, taking Cami's hand. "The new group of soldiers from the integration program are coming in soon and it's our turn to do the tour."

"Oh, yay," Cami said sarcastically.

"Oh, come on; at least they've all started to get past being star-struck every time they see a confirmed vampire."

"Yes, if I had one more person ask to see my fangs I was going to end up using them," Cami said in irritation as they walked away.

"Hey, your dad will be here at seven for my check up; will you be back in time to see him? I think your mom is coming, too," Alexa called after them.

"Sure, we'll make it back," Jared answered over his shoulder.

"We should head inside, too," Rachel said softly. "Someone is overdue for his nap." Martinez turned to reveal Jackson's sleeping face lying against his shoulder.

Alexa smiled and waved as the family made their way to their cottage.

"So, Amor, how are you and my sons feeling today?" Ethan asked, sliding onto the bench to sit beside her ,while keeping one hand resting on her stomach.

"We feel amazing, Mr. Kellar. I don't think life could be any better than it is right now."

"I have to disagree with you. I know that it can be," he said, his tone serious as he ran his finger down her cheek. She looked at him curiously, wondering where he was going with that. "Every day I get with you is better than the last," he added with a wide grin that earned him a long kiss.

Alexa pulled back and looked up into his eyes that were staring back at her with so much love and admiration. In such a short time, they'd been through hell and back, through sickness and health, and were even parted by death; yet there they were, together and stronger than ever. As she'd moved aimlessly through her lonely human life, Alexa had always believed that fate was working against her, but in the end, with her new life full of love, family, and happiness, it seemed that fate had always been on her side.

The Fate Series

Choices of Fate - Book 1

Redemption of Fate - Book 2

Absolution of Fate - Book 3

For more information on titles by S. Simone Chavous
please visit

www.ssimonechavous.com

About the Author

S. Simone Chavous spent seven years as a tax accountant before deciding to pursue her true passion as an author. She lives in northern Indiana with her boyfriend, two beautiful daughters, and their rambunctious vizsla, Lily.

To learn more about S. Simone, please visit:
www.ssimonechavous.com

or connect with her on Facebook at
www.facebook.com/ssimonechavous